Praise for *Wetlands:*

"A warning: do not start reading this book on your lunch break. . . . A sharply written, taboo-busting black comedy, both gross and engrossing."   —*New Statesman* (UK)

"While certainly not for the squeamish . . . [*Wetlands*] has administered CPR to feminism."   —*Bust*

"Not since Germaine Greer's *The Female Eunuch* have readers and critics had such a Rohrschach test for their body issues."
—*Bookslut*

"Brave and hilarious. In a world where women's bodies are supposed to be nipped, tucked, shaved, and douched, *Wetlands* is a much needed antidote."   —Jessica Valenti, author of
The Purity Myth and *Full Frontal Feminism*

"Every once in a while, the novel, which keeps defaulting to its genteel, overmannered self, needs a purgative, and Charlotte Roche's *Wetlands* is it."   —*San Francisco Chronicle*

"A stomach-churning read . . . Helen is witty, charming, and endearingly weird. . . . [*Wetlands*] has certainly struck a nerve."
—*The National Post* (Canada)

"A scatological counterattack to our ultra-sanitized world. Scandalous, compelling, and altogether disturbing, this is a new erotic literary classic."   —*Curve*

"If you ever wondered what you'd be like if you weren't shy, polite, tolerant, modest, sexually repressed, logical, and constrained by modern standards of hygiene, this may be the book for you."   —*The Guardian* (UK)

"[Reading *Wetlands*] left us with that not-so-fresh feeling."
—*Time Out New York*

"An upfront riposte to the evils of 'raunch culture'—a Teutonic paean to all things female, hairy and swampy . . . Written with pervy poise, this tongue-in-cheek polemic wrestles with any number of taboos."   —*The Independent* (UK)

"A bold, brash manifesto of contemporary feminine rebellion. Charlotte Roche is the long-lost love child of Anaïs Nin and Henry Miller."   —Kevin Keck, author of *Oedipus Wrecked*

"If *Wetlands* helps women take away a moment of understanding that we're all sort of dirty and weird and sexual and that *that's okay*, then, fuck it, this should be required reading."   —*Jezebel*

"Roche has created a female lead that is likeable and funny, flawed and idiosyncratic. . . . [*Wetlands*] is an easy page-turner of a read, with a [heroine] who doesn't conform to mainstream ideas of femininity, and a great mixture of the gross and erotic."
—*Subtext Magazine*

"*Wetlands* is at times difficult to read, but that is all the more reason to read it. Female readers will be compelled to analyze their reaction to the gross-outs of the novel, and what it says about their own ideas about femininity, but I almost hope the readers are more often male. Women: give this book to a man who needs to read it!"
—Jessica Cutler, author of *The Washingtonienne*

"Using language explicit enough to make the Mayflower Madam blush . . . the sassy if confessional tone [of *Wetlands*] introduces a twenty-first century Lolita whose bravado is slowly chipped away. . . . Intense . . . Exhilarating, moving, sad, and scary."
—*Library Journal*

WETLANDS

WETLANDS

Charlotte Roche

Translated from the German by Tim Mohr

Grove Press
New York

Originally published in Germany under the title *Feuchtgebiete*

Printed in the United States of America

ISBN-13: 978-0-8021-4469-0

Grove Press
an imprint of Grove/Atlantic, Inc.
841 Broadway
New York, NY 10003

Distributed by Publishers Group West

www.groveatlantic.com

10 11 12   10 9 8 7 6 5 4 3 2 1

For Martin

I place a lot of importance on the care of the elderly within a family. I'm also a child of divorce, and like all children of divorce I want to see my parents back together. When my parents eventually need to be taken care of, all I have to do is stick their new partners in nursing homes and then I'll look after the two of them myself—at home. I'll put them together in their matrimonial bed until they die.

WETLANDS

As far back as I can remember, I've had hemorrhoids. For many, many years I thought I couldn't tell anyone. After all, only grandfathers get hemorrhoids. I always thought they were very unladylike. I've been to Dr. Fiddel, my proctologist, about them so many times. But he always said to leave them there as long as they didn't hurt. And they didn't. They just itched. And for that he gave me a zinc salve.

For exterior itching, you squeeze a hazelnut-sized dollop from the tube onto your finger with the shortest nail and rub it onto your rosette. The tube's also got a pointed attachment with lots of holes in it that allows you to shove it up your ass and squeeze salve out to quell the itchiness inside.

Before I had the salve I would scratch at my butthole in my sleep so much that I'd wake up in the morning with a brown stain in my underwear the size of the top of a cork. That's how much it itched, and that's how deep I'd stick my finger in. So yes, I'd say it's very unladylike.

My hemorrhoids look strange. Over the years they've worked their way farther and farther out. All around the rosette now there are cloud-shaped lobes of skin that almost look like the arms of a sea anemone. Dr. Fiddel calls it cauliflower.

He says removing it would be strictly an aesthetic move. He'll only take it off if someone is really burdened by it. A good reason for removing it would be if my lover didn't like it, or if the cauliflower gave me anxiety during sex. But I'd never admit that.

If somebody loves me or is even just hot for me, something like the cauliflower shouldn't make a difference. And anyway, I've had very successful anal sex for many years—from the age of fifteen up to now, at eighteen—despite the ever-expanding cauliflower. By very successful I mean that I can come with just a cock up my ass, not being touched anywhere else. Yep, I'm proud of that.

It's also a good way to test whether someone is serious about me. During one of the first few times I have sex with somebody new, I get us into my favorite position: doggy-style, me on all fours with my face down, him behind me with his tongue in my pussy and his nose in my ass. He's got to work his way in there, because the hole is covered with the vegetable. I call this position "stuff your face," and so far nobody has complained.

When you've got something like that on an organ that's so important for sex (is the bum even an organ?), you have to train yourself to relax. This in turn helps enable you to let yourself go and loosen up during, for instance, anal sex.

And since the ass is obviously part of sex for me, it's also subject to the modern shaving regime, along with my pussy, my legs, my underarms, the upper lip, both big toes, and the top of my feet as well. Of course, the upper lip doesn't get shaved but rather plucked, because we all know you'll develop a mustache if you shave it. As a girl you don't want that. I used to be happy enough without all the shaving, but then I started with that crap and now I can't quit.

Back to shaving my ass. Unlike other people, I know exactly what my butthole looks like. I look at it every day in the bathroom. Standing with my bum facing the mirror, legs spread, my hands holding my ass cheeks apart, and my head practically on the floor, I look back between my legs. I shave my ass exactly the same way. Except that I have to let one cheek go in order to hold the razor. The wet blade is put against the cauliflower and then pulled bravely in a straight line outward from the center. Right on out to the middle of the cheek, occasionally leaving behind a stray hair. Since I'm always conflicted about the idea of shaving, I always rush it and end up pressing too hard. Which is exactly how I caused the anal lesion that's the reason I'm lying here in the hospital now. Blame it all on lady-shaving. Feel like Venus. Be a goddess.

Perhaps not everyone knows what an anal lesion is. It's a hairline rip or cut in the skin of your rosette. And if this small open wound gets infected as well—which down there is highly likely—then it hurts like hell. Like with me right now. Turns out your butthole is always in motion. When you talk, laugh, cough, walk, sleep, and, above all else, when you go to the bathroom. But I only realized this once it started to hurt.

The swollen hemorrhoids are also pushing with all their strength against the razor wound, ripping the lesion open even farther and causing the worst pain I've ever experienced. By far. In second place is the pain I felt run down my spine—*ratatatatat*—the time my father accidentally slammed the hatchback door of our car on my back. The third worst pain I've ever felt was when I ripped out my nipple ring taking off a sweater. That's why my right nipple looks like a snake's tongue now.

Back to my bum. In excruciating pain I made my way from school to the hospital and showed my cut to every doctor. Immediately I got a bed in the proctology unit—or do you call it the internal-medicine unit? Internal medicine sounds better than specifying "ass unit." Don't want to make other people envious. Maybe we can just generalize with internal medicine. I'll ask about it later, when the pain is gone. Anyway, now I'm not allowed to move. I just lie here in the fetal position. With my skirt hiked up and my underpants pulled down, ass toward the door. That way anyone who enters the room immediately knows what the story is. It must look really infected. Everyone who comes in says, "Ooh."

And they talk about pus and an engorged blister that's hanging out of the wound on my butthole. I picture the blister like the skin on the neck of one of those tropical birds that puffs its throat out when trying to mate. A shimmering, inflated, red-blue sac. The next proctologist who comes in says curtly, "Hello, the name is Dr. Notz."

Then he jams something up my asshole. The pain bores its way up my spine and into my brain. I nearly pass out. After a few seconds of pain I feel a wet squishiness and cry out, "Ow! Give me some warning. What the hell was that?"

His response: "My thumb. You'll have to excuse me, but with that big blister there I couldn't see anything."

What a way to introduce yourself.

"And now? What do you see?"

"We've got to operate immediately. Have you eaten anything today?"

"How could I with this pain?"

"Good. General anesthesia then. It's better given the situation."

I'm happy, too. I don't want to be conscious for something like this.

"What exactly are you going to do during the operation?"

The conversation is already straining me. It's tough to concentrate on anything but the pain.

"We'll make a wedge-shaped incision to cut out the infected tissue."

"I can't really picture that—wedge-shaped? Can you draw a picture for me?"

Apparently the esteemed Dr. Notz hasn't often been asked by patients to sketch a diagram right before an operation. He wants to leave, glances at the door, stifles a sigh.

Then he pulls a silver pen out of his chest pocket. It looks heavy. Expensive. He looks around for a piece of paper to draw on. I can't help him and hope he doesn't expect me to. Any movement hurts. I close my eyes. There's rustling and I hear him ripping a piece of paper out of something. I have to open my eyes—I'm anxious to see the drawing. He holds the piece of paper in his palm and scribbles with the pen. Then he presents his creation. I read: savoy cabbage in cream sauce. No way. He's ripped the paper out of the hospital menu. I turn the paper around. He's drawn a circle. I figure it's supposed to be my butthole. And out of the circle a triangular wedge has been cut, as if someone has made off with a piece of cake.

Aha, got it. Thanks, Dr. Notz. Ever thought about putting all that talent into a career as an artist? The sketch doesn't help me at all. Though I'm still no better informed, I don't ask any more questions. He isn't interested in helping enlighten me.

"Surely you could cut out the cauliflower with just a little flick of the wrist?"

"It'll be done."

He walks out, leaving me lying in the puddle of water from the blister. I'm alone. And worried about the operation. I think of general anesthesia as something dangerous, as if every second patient never wakes up. I feel courageous for going ahead with it. The anesthesiologist comes in next.

The sandman. He pulls up a low stool and sits down with his face right in front of mine. He speaks softly and has a lot more compassion for my situation than Dr. Notz. He asks how old I am. If I were under eighteen there would have to be a legal guardian here. But I'm not. I tell him I've come of legal age this year. He looks incredulously into my eyes. I know. Nobody ever believes it; I look younger. I know this drill. I put on my serious you-can-trust-me face and lock eyes with him. His gaze changes. He believes me. On with the discussion.

He explains how the anesthesia works. I'll count and then just fall asleep at some point without even noticing. He'll sit by my head throughout the operation, monitor my breathing, and check that the anesthesia is agreeing with me. Aha. So this sitting-too-close-to-my-face thing is an occupational hazard. Most people don't notice anyway—they're knocked out. And he's probably supposed to be as unobtrusive as possible and hunker down close to the patient's head so as not to disturb the real doctors. Poor guy. The standard position while practicing his trade? Squatting.

He's brought a contract that I'm supposed to sign. It says the operation could result in incontinence. I ask how it could affect my pissing. He grins and says this refers to anal incontinence. Never heard of it. But suddenly I realize what this means: "You mean I might lose control of my sphincter muscles and then I could just crap myself anytime and anyplace and would need a diaper and stink all the time?"

The sandman: "Yes, but that rarely happens. Sign here, please."

I sign it. What else am I supposed to do? If that's what it takes to have the surgery. I can't exactly go home and operate on myself.

Oh, man. Please, dear nonexistent God, don't let this happen. I'd be wearing a diaper at age eighteen. You're not supposed to need those until you're eighty. It would also mean I'd only have managed to live fourteen years of my life without diapers. And you certainly don't look cool in them.

"Dear anesthesiologist, would it be possible for me to see what they cut away during the operation? I don't like the idea that a part of me could end up in the trash along with aborted fetuses and appendixes without my being able to picture it. I want to hold it in my hand and examine it."

"If that's what you want, then sure."

"Thanks." He sticks a catheter into my arm and secures everything with surgical tape. This is where they'll pump in the anesthesia later. He says that in a few minutes a nurse will come to take me to surgery. Now the anesthesiologist too leaves me lying in the puddle of moisture from my blister and walks out.

The thought of anal incontinence worries me.

Dear nonexistent God, if I manage to get out of here without anal incontinence, I'll stop doing all the things that give me a bad conscience. Like the game I play with my friend Corinna where we run through the city drunk and grab people's eyeglasses, break them, and then chuck them into the street.

We have to run quickly—some people get so pissed off that they come after us really fast even without their glasses.

The game is stupid anyway because we always sober up from all the excitement and adrenaline. Big waste of money. Afterward we always have to start from scratch again getting drunk.

Actually, I'd like to give that game up anyway— sometimes at night I dream of the faces of the people whose glasses we've just plucked off. It's as if we've ripped off a body part.

I'll give that one up right now, and I'll try to come up with a list of some other things.

Maybe if it's absolutely necessary I'll give up the hookers. That would be a major sacrifice, though. It would be great if giving up the glasses game would suffice.

I've decided to be the best patient this hospital has ever had. I'm going to be extra nice to the overworked nurses and doctors. I'll clean up my own messes. Like the fluid from my blister. There's an open box of rubber gloves on the windowsill. Obviously for examinations. Did Notz have one on when he popped the blister on my ass? Shit, I didn't notice. Next to the carton of rubber gloves is a big translucent-plastic container. Tupperware for a giant. Maybe there's something in there I can use to clean myself up. My bed is up against the window. Slowly, gingerly, I stretch myself out a little without moving my infected bum and manage to grab it. I pull the container onto my bed. Ouch. Lifting it and pulling it tenses my stomach muscles, sending a knife of pain into the infection. I pause. Close my eyes. Breathe deeply. Lie still. Wait for the pain to subside. Eyes open. Okay.

Now I can open the container. What excitement. It's filled to the brim with giant hygienic wipes, adult diapers, disposable underwear, toweling, and bed covers that are plastic on one side and cloth on the other.

I would like to have had one of those under me when Notz came in. Then the bed wouldn't be all wet. Not very comfortable. I need two of them now. One, cloth side down over the puddle. It'll soak it up. But then I'd be laying on plastic. Don't like that. So another one with its plastic side down—plastic on plastic—and the cloth side up. Well done, Helen. Despite the hellish pain, you are your own best nurse.

Anyone who can take care of herself so well will definitely recuperate quickly. I'll have to be a bit more hygienic here in the hospital than I am outside in my normal life.

Hygiene's not a major concern of mine.

At some point I realized that boys and girls are taught differently about how to keep their intimate regions clean. My mother placed great importance on the hygiene of my pussy but none at all on that of my brother's penis. He's allowed to piss without wiping and to let the last few drops dribble into his underwear.

Washing your pussy is considered a deadly serious science in our home. It's made out to be extremely difficult to keep a pussy really clean. Which is nonsense, of course. A little water, a little soap, scrub-scrub. Done.

Just don't wash too much. For one thing because of the all-important flora of the pussy. But also because of the taste and scent of the pussy, which is so important during sex. Don't want to get rid of that. I've experimented with long periods of not washing my pussy. My aim is to get its enticing scent to waft lightly out of my pants, even through thick jeans or ski pants. Men won't consciously notice it but it'll register subliminally since we're all just animals who want to mate—preferably with someone who smells like pussy.

Then, when you're flirting, you can't help smiling the whole time because you know what's filling the air with that deliciously sweet scent. It's what perfume is supposed to accomplish. We're always told that perfume has an erotic effect on those around us. But why not use our own much more powerful perfume? In reality we're all turned on by the scents of pussy, cock, and sweat. Most people have just been alienated from their bodies and trained to think that anything natural stinks and anything artificial smells nice. When a woman wearing perfume passes me on the street, it makes me sick to my stomach. No matter how subtle it is. What is she hiding? Women spray perfume in public toilets after they've taken a shit, too. They think it makes everything smell pleasant again. But I still smell the shit. For me, the smell of plain old shit or piss is better than the disgusting perfumes people buy.

Even worse than women spraying perfume in public toilets is a new invention that seems to be spreading fast.

You go to the bathroom at a restaurant or train station and as you pull the stall door closed behind you, you're misted from above. The first time it happened I was really horrified. I thought someone had flicked water on me from another stall. But then I looked up and saw a dispenser attached above the top of the door. It's actually designed to spray innocent bathroom users with sickeningly sweet disinfectant as soon as they close the door. On your hair, on your clothes, on your face. If that doesn't constitute rape by hygiene fanatics I don't know what does.

I use my smegma the way others use their vials of perfume. I dip my finger into my pussy and dab a little slime behind my earlobes. It works wonders from the moment you greet someone with a kiss on each cheek. Another rule my mother had about pussies was that they get infected much more easily than penises. That they're much more vulnerable to fungus and mold and whatnot. Which is why girls should never sit down on an unfamiliar or public toilet seat. I was taught to piss in an upright crouch, hovering above the rim, never touching the icky pee-pee basin at all. But I've figured out that a lot of the things I was taught aren't true.

I've turned myself into a walking laboratory of pussy hygiene. I enjoy plopping myself down on any dirty toilet seat anywhere. That's not all. I rub the entire seat with my pussy before I sit down, going once around with a graceful gyration of my hips. When I press my pussy onto the seat it makes a smacking noise and then it sucks up all the pubic hairs, droplets, splotches, and puddles of various shades and consistencies. I've been doing this on every sort of toilet for four years now. My favorites are the ones at highway rest stops where there's just one toilet shared by men and women. And I've never had a single infection. My gynecologist, Dr. Broekert, can confirm that.

Once there was a time when I did think my pussy was infected. Whenever I went to the bathroom, sat down, and let my sphincter muscles relax so the piss could come out, I would notice afterward when I looked down—which I like to do—that there was a lovely, big, soft, white clump of slime in the water. With strings of champagne bubbles rising from it.

I have to admit that I'm very wet all day long—I could change my underwear several times a day. But I don't. I like to let it collect. Back to the clump of slime. Was it possible that I'd been sick all along, and that this slimy gunk was the result of a fungal infection of the pussy I'd contracted from all my toilet experiments?

Dr. Broekert was able to allay my fears. It was the result of a healthy, very-active slime-producing mucous membrane. That's not how he put it. But that's what he meant.

I keep close track of my bodily secretions. The whole active mucous-membrane thing used to make me proud when I was younger, hooking up with boys. They might have barely touched my labia with a finger, but inside there was a Slip 'N Slide ready to go.

One boyfriend always sang while we were messing around: "By the rivers of Babylon . . ." These days I could make a business out of it, filling little containers for dry women who have problems producing mucus. It's definitely better to get the real thing than to use some artificial lube.

That way it smells like pussy, too! But maybe women would only be willing to do this with someone they knew—some might be grossed out by a stranger's slime. You could always try it out. Maybe with a dry friend.

I really like to smell and eat my smegma. For as long as I can remember, I've been fascinated with my pussy's creases. All the things you can find in there. I have long hair—on my head—and sometimes I'll find a stray hair lodged between the folds of my pussy. It's exciting to pull the hair out very slowly and to feel it moving in the various places it has twisted its way into. It annoys me when this sensation is over; I wish I had even longer hair so the feeling would last longer.

It's a rare pleasure. Like another thing I get a kick out of: when I'm alone in the bathtub and I have to fart, I try to get the air bubbles to glide up between my pussy lips. It doesn't happen very often—even less often than with the long hairs—but when it does, the bubbles feel like hard balls trying to bore their way between my warm, squishy lips. When it happens—let's say once a month—my whole abdomen tingles and my pussy itches so much I have to scratch it with my long fingernails until I come. When my pussy itches I have to scratch it real hard. I scratch up and down between the inner labia—which I call the dewlaps—and the outer labia—which I call the ladyfingers—and at some point I fold back the dewlaps to the right and left so I can scratch right down the middle. I spread my legs wide, until the hip joints crack, so the warm bathwater can flow into my hole. Right as I'm about to come, I pinch my clit—which I call my snail tail. That makes me come so much harder. Yep, that's how it's done.

Back to smegma. I looked up in the dictionary exactly what smegma is. My best friend Corrina told me one time that only men have smegma.

So what's this between my lips and in my underwear?

That's what I thought, but not what I said. I was afraid to say it. But there in the dictionary was a long explanation of what smegma is. That's what it's called in women, too, by the way. So ha! One sentence has stuck with me to this day: "Only through inadequate hygiene can smegma accumulate to a level visible to the naked eye."

Excuse me? That's outrageous. An accumulation of smegma is definitely visible to me with the naked eye at the end of the day no matter how thoroughly I rinse the folds of my pussy with soapy water in the morning.

So what do they mean? Are you supposed to wash yourself multiple times during the day? Anyway, it's good to have a juicy pussy. It's extremely helpful for certain things. The concept of "inadequate hygiene" is flexible—like a pussy. So there.

I take one of the adult diapers out of the translucent-plastic container. Oh man, they're huge. They've got a big, thick square pad in the middle and four thin, plastic tabs to secure at the waist. They'd easily fit around a fat old man—that's how big they are. It's not something I want to need so early in life. Please. There's a knock at the door.

In comes a smiling nurse with his hair sticking up like a cockatoo. "Hello, Miss Memel. My name is Robin. I can see you're already getting familiar with the supplies you'll need during the next few days. You're going to have surgery on your anus, an unhygienic area—the most unhygienic part of the body, in fact. With the items in the container you'll be able to tend to your wound all by yourself after the operation. We recommend that at least once a day you get in the shower and use the showerhead to rinse out the wound. It's best to make sure you spray water up inside. With a little practice, it's easy. It'll be a lot less painful for you to clean the wound that way than to wipe it with towels. After you've rinsed, just pat it dry with a washcloth. I've also got a sedative here. You can take it now. It makes the transition to general anesthesia easier. We're just about ready—it should be some ride."

None of this sounds like a problem. I certainly know my way around a showerhead. And I know just how to get the spray inside. As Robin pushes me through the hallways on my rolling bed and I watch the long fluorescent lightbulbs pass overhead, I discreetly reach down under the sheet and put my hand on my pubic mound to settle myself down before the operation. I divert my attention from the fear by thinking of how I would get myself off with the showerhead when I was younger.

At first I'd just aim the streams of water at my pussy; later I'd hold the ladyfingers aside so the water would hit the dewlaps and snail tail. The harder the better. It should really sting. At some point a few jets of water actually shot up inside my pussy. And I realized this was my thing. To let it fill up and—just as nice—to let it all run out again.

I sit cross-legged in the tub, leaning back with my butt slightly raised. Then I push all the lips to the side, where they belong, and very slowly and carefully slide the thick showerhead in. I don't need any lube—just the thought that I'm about to fill myself up makes my pussy produce plenty of helpful slime. The best lube is Pjur brand because it doesn't clump and it's unscented. I hate scented lubes. It's usually when the showerhead is finally in—which can take a while, because it takes time to stretch out that much—I rotate it so the side the water shoots out of is facing up toward the cervix, toward the spot a guy with a long cock can hit in certain positions. Next the water is turned on, nice and strong. I fold my arms behind my head—both hands are free because my pussy holds the showerhead all by itself—close my eyes, and hum "Amazing Grace."

After what I guess is about four liters, I turn the water off and very carefully pull out the showerhead, letting out as little water as possible. I need the water to get off. I tap the showerhead on my ladyfingers, swollen from being held apart, until I come.

It's usually really fast as long as I'm not interrupted. When I feel totally stuffed—like with the water—it only takes a couple of seconds. Once I've come I press one hand on my lower abdomen and stick the other one deep into my pussy with all the fingers splayed out so the water gushes out with the same force as it went in. I usually come again from the water flowing out. It's an effective way to calm myself. After the big rush of water, spurts of water will still come out for several hours, so I have to line my underwear with sheets of toilet paper—if it soaked through my pants it would look as if I'd wet myself. I don't want that.

Another sanitation device that's perfect for this sort of thing is the bidet. My mother always stressed the importance of quickly freshening up with a bidet after sex. Why should I?

If I fuck someone, I'm proud to have his sperm in every crevice of my body, whether that's on my thighs, on my stomach, or wherever else he may have shot his load. Why the idiotic washing afterward? If you find cocks, cum, or smegma disgusting, you might as well forget about sex. I love it when sperm dries on my skin, when it crusts and flakes off.

When I jerk somebody off, I always make sure that some cum gets on my hand. I run my fingers through it and let it dry under my long nails. That way, later in the day, I can reminisce about my good fuck partner by biting my nails and getting bits of the hardened cum to play with in my mouth; I chew on it and, after tasting it and letting it slowly dissolve, I swallow it. It's an invention I'm very proud of: the memorable-sex bonbon.

The same can be done, of course, with cum that ends up in the pussy. Just don't wash it away with a bidet! Instead, carry it proudly. To school, for instance. Hours after sex it'll ooze nice and warm out of your pussy—a little treat. I may be sitting in a classroom, but my thoughts are back where the cum came from: while the teacher is going on about philosophical attempts to prove the existence of God, I sit there smiling blissfully in my little puddle of sperm. The intermingling of bodily fluids between my legs always makes me happy, and I text the source: "Your warm cum is running out of me—thanks!"

My thoughts return to the bidet. I wanted to spend a few minutes reminiscing about the way I manage to fill myself up with the bidet. But there's no time. We've arrived in the surgery prep room. I can continue that line of thought later. My anesthesiologist is already waiting for us. He attaches a bag of fluid to the IV tube in my arm, hangs it upside down from a rolling stand, and says I should start counting.

Robin, the friendly nurse, wishes me luck and leaves. One, two . . .

I wake up in the recovery room. People are always a bit out of sorts when they wake up from general anesthesia. I think recovery rooms were created to spare relatives from witnessing this.

I'm awoken by my own babbling. What was I saying? Don't know. My whole body is shaking. Slowly the gears in my mind begin to turn. What am I doing here? Did something happen to me? I want to smile to try to hide my sense of helplessness even though there's nobody else in the room. My lips are so dry that the corner of my mouth cracks when I do smile. My asshole! That's why I'm here. It had cracked, too. My hand fumbles for my bum. I feel a huge bandage stretched across both ass cheeks. Through that I feel a thick knob. Oh man, I hope that knob isn't part of my body. Hopefully it's something that will come off with the rest of the bandaging. I'm in one of those embarrassing, apron-like hospital gowns. They love these gowns in hospitals.

It has sleeves and from the front makes you look like a tree-top angel. But it's completely backless except for a little bow tied back there. Why does this piece of clothing even exist? I mean, sure, if you're lying down they can put one on you without having to lift you. But I was lying on my stomach for the operation so they could get at my ass. Does that mean I was essentially naked for the duration of the operation? That's not good. I'm sure they talk about the way you look. And you hear it and remember it subconsciously even though you're knocked out—maybe someday down the road you'll go nuts as a result of the comments and nobody will understand why.

This airy feeling on my backside reminds me of a re-curring nightmare I had as a child. Elementary school. I'm waiting at the bus stop. Just as I often forgot to take my pajamas off before putting on my jeans, today I've forgot-ten to put underwear on beneath my skirt. You don't no-tice that kind of thing at home as a kid. But you'd rather die than have people discover in public that you're bare-assed under your skirt. And this was at exactly the age when the boys think it's funny to lift girls' skirts.

Robin walks in. He speaks very deliberately, saying everything went smoothly. He pushes my gurney into an ele-vator and then along hallways, always slamming his fist on the game-show buttons that open the automatic doors. Oh, Robin. The lingering effects of the anesthesia make for a hypnotic ride. I use the time to find out about my asshole. It's a funny feeling that Robin knows more about it than I do. He's got a clipboard with every detail about me and my ass on it. I'm feeling talkative and all kinds of jokes about bum surgery occur to me. He says I'm so relaxed and funny because the anesthesia's still affecting me. He parks my bed back in my room and says he could talk to me for ages but that he has other patients he needs to check on. Too bad.

"If you need pain medication, just press the call button."

"Where's the skirt and underwear I had on before the operation?"

He walks to the foot of my bed and lifts the sheet. The skirt is carefully folded there with my underpants on top of it.

This is the situation my mother always feared. The underwear is folded with the crotch facing up. Right side in, not inside out. But I can still see a shiny stain where pussy juice has soaked through and dried. My mom thinks the single most important thing for a woman going to the hospital to do is to wear clean underwear. Her primary justification for her ridiculously obsessive approach to clean undies: If you get run over and end up in the hospital, they take your clothes off. Including your underwear. Oh my God. And if they see any evidence of your pussy's totally normal discharge—oh my, can you imagine?

I think mom pictures everyone in the hospital going around talking about her, saying what a dirty whore Mrs. Memel is. Saying her well-put-together exterior is nothing but a lie.

Her dying thought at the scene of an accident would be: How long have I been wearing these panties? Are there any wet spots on them?

The first thing doctors and EMTs do with a bleeding accident victim, before starting to resuscitate? They have a peek at the blood-soaked underwear so they know what kind of woman they've got on their hands.

From the wall behind me Robin pulls out a cable with a call button on the end of it. He lays it on the pillow next to my face. I won't need that.

I look around my room. The walls are painted light green —so light it's barely perceptible. Supposed to be calming. Or optimistic.

To the left of my bed is a built-in wardrobe. I don't have anything to put in it, but someone will bring me things soon, I'm sure. Beyond the wardrobe the room goes on around, probably to the bathroom—or let's call it the shower room.

Between my bed and the wardrobe is a rolling metal nightstand with a drawer. It's extra tall so you can get at it from the high hospital bed.

To the right is a long bank of windows hung with white, see-through curtains that are weighted at the bottom to keep them hanging crisply. They've got to look neat and straight. Like concrete. They mustn't billow in the breeze if the window is open. On the sill is the container of diapers and, next to it, a box with one hundred pairs of rubber gloves in it. It says so on the box. Though there's probably fewer than that in there now.

On the wall opposite me is a framed poster—you can see the little metal tabs that hold the glass. It's a photo of a tree-lined avenue, and written in yellow letters at the top it says, *Walk with Jesus*. What—take him for a stroll?

A small crucifix hangs over the doorway. Someone has decorated it with a bough. Why do they do that? The boughs are always from the same kind of plant. The kind with little arched leaves, dark green, with an artificial shine to them. The boughs always look like they're made out of plastic, but they always turn out to be real. I think they come from some kind of hedge.

Why do they stick pieces of greenery on crosses? The poster and the crucifix have got to go. I'll convince mom to take them down. I'm already looking forward to that discussion. Mom's a practicing Catholic. Wait. I've forgotten something. Up high is a TV. I hadn't looked up there. It's suspended in a metal frame and tipped way down toward me. It looks as if it could fall on me at any moment. I'll ask Robin to shake it later. Just to make sure it's secure. If there's a TV, there must be a remote—or do I have to get somebody to turn it on and off for me? Maybe it's in the drawer. I reach over and pull it open and am suddenly aware of my ass. Careful, Helen. Don't do anything stupid.

The remote is in a plastic compartment in the drawer. Everything's cool. Except the anesthesia is wearing off. Do I need to ring and ask for painkillers already?

Maybe it won't be that bad. Right, I'll wait a bit and see how I feel. I'll try to keep my mind on something else. Like, say, the last unicorn. That won't work. I clench my teeth. My mind is fixated on my wounded ass. I'm tensing up all over. Especially in my shoulders. My good mood has disappeared. Robin was right. I don't want to come across as a whiner, though—especially after yapping so much to Robin. I can hold out a little longer. I close my eyes. I put one hand gently on my bandaged ass and the other on the call button. I lie there and the pain throbs. The anesthesia is getting weaker and weaker. The wound burns. My muscles cramp. The throbbing gets faster.

I push the button and wait. An eternity. I panic. The pain is getting worse, stabbing at my sphincter like a knife. They must have stretched the sphincter wide open. Of course. How else would they get in there. Down my throat? Oh God. The hands of a full-grown man went into my rectum and went to town with scalpels and retractors and suture thread. The pain isn't directly on the wound but all around it. A blown sphincter.

He's finally arrived.

"Robin?"

"Yes?"

"Do they stretch your butthole open wide enough to fit multiple hands into it?"

"Yes, I'm afraid so. That will be the source of most of the pain when the anesthesia wears off in a few minutes."

Hmm. In a few minutes? I need pain medication right now. The thought that it might take a while for painkillers to work scares me so much that I think I'm going throw up. I've held out against the pain too long and now I'll have to wait ages for this shit on my ass to stop hurting. I've got to learn to give in to pain and become a patient who'd rather ring too soon for medication than have to make it through the minutes it takes for the stuff to kick in. There's no medal for holding out against pain, Helen. My asshole has been fatally distended.

It feels as if the hole is as big around as my entire ass. There's no way it will ever close normally again. I think they purposefully inflicted additional pain during the operation.

I was in this same hospital a few years ago. It was the greatest acting job of my life. I was failing French class and was supposed to take an exam the next day. I hadn't studied and had been skipping class. I had faked being sick for the previous exam. I had pretended I had a migraine so mom would give me a note. This time it had to be something more convincing. I just needed some time to study.

An excused absence would mean I could make up the exam some other time. First thing in the morning I told my mom I had palpitations in my lower left abdomen. And that they were getting worse. Mom started to worry because she knew this was a sign of appendicitis. Even though the appendix is on the right side. I know that, too. I started to double over in pain. She drove me straight to the pediatrician. I still go to the same doctor I went to as a child. It's closer to home. He laid me on a stretcher and began to press on my abdomen. He pressed on the left side and I shrieked in pain. He pressed on the right and I didn't make a sound.

"It's unmistakable. Acute appendicitis. You've got to take your daughter to the hospital right away. There's no time to stop off at home for her pajamas. You can drop them off later. This kid's got to get to the hospital. If it ruptures it'll infect the entire body and she'll need a blood transfusion." I thought to myself, What kid?

Off to the hospital. This one. Upon arrival I put on the same show. Left, right, all the right reactions. Like a game. Emergency operation. They cut me open and find an appendix that's not infected or swollen at all. They take it out anyway. You don't need it. And if they left it in and sewed you up, you might just come back at some stage with real appendicitis. Which would be doubly annoying. But they didn't tell me they took it out. My mother did.

When she caught me lying another time, she said: "I can't believe anything you say. You lied to me and all the doctors just to get out of a French exam. They took an uninfected appendix out of you."

"How do you know that?"

"Mothers know everything. The doctors told me outside the operating room. They had never encountered anything like it before. So I know what a liar you are."

At least I knew it was out. Before that conversation with my mom I figured the doctors had opened me up, seen it wasn't infected, and left it in. So I had always worried I might really get appendicitis. And what could you say then, when you'd supposedly already had appendicitis? So that's what had happened. Good to know. A lot of needless hours of worrying. Right after you've had your appendix taken out, it hurts incredibly badly to laugh, to walk, to stand, to do much of anything, because it feels as if the stitches are going to rip open. I tensed and curled up just like now with my ass. Is it possible the doctors recognized my name? Did it cause a sensation in the hospital back then—that a girl would endure an operation just to trick her teacher? Did they go out of their way to make this operation particularly painful—oops, I slipped—as payback? Am I paranoid because of the pain? Because of the painkillers? What is going on? It hurts so bad. Robin. Bring the pills.

Here he comes. He hands me two tablets and says something. I can't concentrate. I'm writhing in pain. I slurp the pills down. Please, let them work fast. Now. To calm myself down, I put my hand on my pubic mound again. I always did this as a kid, too. But back then I didn't know it was called a pubic mound.

As far as I'm concerned, it's the most important part of the whole body. Nice and warm. Perfectly positioned for your hand to reach. My center. I stick my hand into my underwear and run my hand around. This is the best way to put myself to sleep.

I root around like a squirrel down there, and just as I'm falling asleep I have the impression there's a log of crap poking out of my ass. The bandages feel exactly like that. I dream that I'm walking across a wide field. A field of parsnips. I can see a man in the distance. A Nordic walker. One of those guys who hikes with a pair of ski-pole-like walking sticks. I think: Look, Helen, a man with four legs.

He approaches and I can see a giant cock is hanging out of his form-fitting sports leggings. I think: Nope, a man with five legs.

He walks past me and I turn and watch him go. It pleases me to see he's pulled his pants down in the back and a huge log of crap is hanging out of his ass, bigger even than his cock. I think: Wow, six legs. I come to and I'm thirsty and aching. The hand on my pubic mound wanders to the back to feel my wound. I want to see what they did back there. How can I have a look? I can look at my pussy if I bend way forward, but I've never been able to see my own ass. A mirror? No, a camera. Mom needs to bring me the camera.

Will she be here when I wake up? Message.

"It's me. Can you bring the camera when you come? And can you wrap up the bulbs in my room without break-ing the shoots? And bring the empty glasses, too, please. But hide them when you come in, Okay? You're not allowed to have anything but cut flowers here. Thanks. See you soon. Oh yeah, can you also bring about thirty toothpicks? Thanks."

I grow avocado trees. Besides fucking, it's my only hobby. As a kid avocados were my favorite fruit or vegetable—whatever they are. Cut in half with a dollop of mayonnaise in the hole where the pit's been removed. And a bunch of hot paprika powder sprinkled on top. I would play with the pits afterward. My mother would always say kids didn't need toys—a rotten tomato or an avocado pit did just fine.

At first the pit is shiny and slimy from the avocado oil. I like to rub it on the backs of my hands and up and down my arms. Spread the slime all over. Then you have to dry the pit.

If you leave it on the radiator it only takes a few days. Once the moisture has dried, I run the soft, dark-brown pit across my lips. When they're dry they feel so soft. I like to do it for minutes on end, with my eyes closed. It's like when I would run my dry lips across the greasy leather cover of the pommel horse in the school gym—until someone would interrupt me. "Helen, what are you doing? Stop that."

Or until the other kids would laugh at me. Then you spare yourself the embarrassment by doing it only during the few moments you can sneak into the gym alone. It's about as soft as my ladyfingers when they're freshly shaved.

You've got to peel the brown shell off the pit. To do that I stick my thumbnail into the shell and keep cracking it. Just be careful not to let any pieces of the shell jab under your nail.

That hurts and it's hard to get the pieces out even with a needle and tweezers. And trying to finish ripping open the shell with splinters under your nail hurts worse than the initial pain of them getting jammed in there in the first place. It'll leave ugly bloody marks under your nail, too. The blood doesn't stay red, either. It turns brown. It takes a long time for it to grow out. In the meantime your nail looks like a sheet of floating ice with a piece of driftwood frozen into it. Once the shell's completely removed you can see the pleasant color of the pit—either light yellow or sometimes pale pink.

Then I hit it with a hammer. But not so hard that it crushes. After that I put it in the freezer for a few hours to simulate winter. Once you've had enough of winter, you pull it out and insert three toothpicks into the pit. Then you suspend it in water in a glass, using the toothpicks to hold it at the right height.

An avocado pit looks like an egg. It's got a thick, round end and a more pointed end. The narrower end has to stay above the water. About a third in the air and two-thirds submerged. It'll stay this way for a couple of months.

A slimy film grows on the part of the pit in the water. I find it very inviting. Sometimes I take the pit out of the water and put it inside me. I call it my organic dildo. Obviously I only use organic avocados for my starter pits. Otherwise I'd end up with toxic trees.

You definitely want to take the toothpicks out before you put it inside you. Thanks to my well-trained pelvic muscles I can shoot it back out afterward. Then it's back into the water with the toothpicks stuck back in. And then you wait.

After a couple of months you'll see a crack in the round end. It'll get wider, a deep crevice in the pit. It looks as if it's about to split in half; then a thick, white, taproot will start to grow out of the bottom. It curls into the bottom of the glass—there's no other direction for it to grow. Once that gets pretty long, if you look closely at the crack on the top side of the pit, you'll see a tiny green sprout starting to grow. Now's the time to transfer it to a pot full of potting soil. Soon a stem grows with big, green leaves.

I'll never get closer to giving birth than this. I looked after that first pit for months. Had it inside me, pushed it out. And I take perfect care of all the avocado trees I've started that way.

As far back as I can remember, I always wanted to have a child. There's a recurring pattern in my family. My great-grandmother, my grandmother, my mother, and me. All first-born. All girls. All neurotic, deranged, and depressed. But I broke the cycle. This year I turned eighteen and I've been waiting for that moment. One day after my birthday— as soon as I didn't need parental approval—I had myself sterilized. Since then the thing my mother says to me so often doesn't sound so threatening: "How much do you want to bet that when you have your first child it's a girl?" Because I'll only be having avocado trees. Apparently you have to wait twenty-five years for a tree to bear fruit. Which is also about how long you have to wait to become a grand-mother. These days.

While I've been lying here thinking happily about my avocado family, the pain has subsided. You always notice when it begins; but you don't notice when it stops. That moment doesn't grab your attention. But I realize the pain is completely gone now. I love painkillers and try to imag-ine what it would have been like to have been born in an-other era when there were no good painkillers. My head is free of pain and now there's room for everything else. I take a few deep breaths and, exhausted, fall asleep. When I open my eyes I see mom leaning over me.

"What are you doing?"

"I'm covering you up. You're lying here totally exposed."

"Leave it the way it is. The sheet's too heavy on my wounded ass, mom. It hurts. It doesn't matter how it looks.

Do you think they haven't seen it here a thousand times before?"

"Then stay that way. Good God."

That reminds me.

"Can you please take down the crucifix over the door? It bugs me."

"No, Helen, I won't do that. Stop being so ridiculous."

"Fine. If you won't help me, I guess I'll have to get up and do it myself."

I start to move one leg off the bed, bluffing that I'm going to stand up, groaning with pain.

"Okay, Okay, I'll do it. Please stay in bed."

No problem.

She uses the lone chair in the room to reach the cross. As she's climbing onto it, she speaks to me in an artificially friendly, sympathetic tone. I feel sorry for her. But it's too late.

"How long have you had this condition?"

What is she talking about? Oh, right. The hemorrhoids.

"Always."

"Not back when I used to bathe you."

"So I got them sometime after I was too old for you to be bathing me."

She climbs back down off the chair, holding the cross in her hand. She looks questioningly at me.

"Put it here in the drawer." I point to the metal nightstand.

"You know, mom, hemorrhoids are hereditary. It's just a question of who I got them from."

She closes the drawer firmly.

"From your father. How was the operation?"

We learned in health class that divorced parents often try to manipulate their kids into taking their respective sides. One parent will bad-mouth the other in front of their kids.

What those bad-mouthing parents fail to realize, though, is that they are always insulting one half of the child. If you consider a child half the mother and half the father.

Children whose mothers constantly insult their fathers will eventually take revenge against their mothers. It all comes back like a boomerang.

So for years the mother has tried to get the child on her side only to have the opposite happen. She's just pushed the child closer to the father.

Our teacher was right.

"I don't know. I wasn't there—they used general anesthesia. They say it all went well. It hurts. Did you bring my avocado pits?"

"Yes, they're over there."

She points to the windowsill. Right next to the diaper container is a box with my beloved pits. Perfect. I can even reach them myself.

"Did you bring the camera?"

She pulls it out of her handbag and puts it on the nightstand.

"What do you need it for here in the hospital?"

"I don't think you should record only the happy moments in life—like birthdays—but also the sad ones, like operations, illness, and death."

"I'm sure it will be a joy for your children and grandchildren to look at an album of those pictures."

I grin. If you only knew, mom.

I hope she'll leave soon. So I can take care of my ass. The only situation in which I would want to spend more time with her would be if there was a legitimate hope of getting her together with dad. He's not coming today. But tomorrow for sure. A hospital with your daughter in it is the perfect place for a family reconciliation. Tomorrow. Today: ass photos.

She says her good-bye and tells me she's left pajamas in the wardrobe. Thanks. How am I supposed to get at them? It doesn't matter—I'd rather lie here bare-bottomed anyway, with all those bandages. Air is good for the wound.

As soon as mom's gone I ring for Robin.

Waiting, waiting. There are other patients, Helen, hard as that is for you to imagine. Here he comes.

"How can I help you, Ms. Memel?"

"I have a question for you. And please don't say no right away."

"Shoot."

"Can you help me . . . actually, can you not call me Ms. Memel. It's too formal for what I want to ask."

"Sure. Happily."

"You're Robin and I'm Helen. Okay. Can you help me take a picture of my ass and the wound on it? I want to see what it looks like."

"Um, let me think for a second—I don't know if I'm allowed."

"Please. Otherwise I'll go crazy. There's no other way for me to figure out what they did back there. You know, Dr. Notz can't even explain it. And it's my ass after all. Please. I can't tell from feeling it. I've got to see it."

"I understand. Interesting. Most patients don't want to know. Okay. What do you want me to do?"

I go to the menu on the camera and set it to close-up. First try will be with no flash. It always looks better. I pull off the outer bandages and the plug of gauze. It takes a while. They've stuffed a lot of gauze in there. I carefully turn on to my other side, my face to the window, and hold my cheeks apart with both hands.

"Robin, now take a picture of the wound as close-up as possible. Hold it steady—the flash is off."

I hear it click once and he shows me the test shot. You can't make anything out. Robin doesn't have a steady hand.

Other talents, though, I'm sure. We'll have to use the flash. And repeat the whole thing.

"Take a few pictures from various angles. Up close and from farther away."

Click, click, click, click. He won't stop.

"That'll do it, Robin, thanks."

He carefully hands me the camera and says, "I've worked here in the proctology unit for ages and I've never been able to see the actual surgical work. So I thank you."

"No, thank you. Can I look at these on my own? And would you do this for me again if it's necessary?"

"Sure."

"You're really cool, Robin."

"You, too, Helen."

He walks out grinning. I stuff the gauze stopper back in.

I'm alone with the device in which the pictures of my wound are saved. I have no idea what to expect. My pulse quickens and I start to sweat with anticipation.

I turn the little wheel mechanism next to the display to the "view pictures" option and hold the camera right in front of my face. It shows a photo of a bloody hole. The flash has cast light deep inside. My ass is wide open. There's nothing to suggest the closure of a sphincter.

I can't make out any crinkled, red-brown skin of a rosette. Actually, I can't make out anything familiar at all. So this is what Notz meant by "wedge-shaped incision." Poor description. I'm appalled at my own asshole—or rather, what's left of it. More hole than ass.

So: I'll never be an ass model. It's just for private use now. Or am I holding the camera wrong? No, that can't be possible—Robin would have held the camera the same way to take the picture.

Yikes. You can look right in. I feel much worse now that I've seen it. The pain comes back suddenly, too. Now that I know what I look like down there, I can't believe the pain will ever go away. There's no skin at all around the entire opening, just red, naked flesh.

I have to let the skin grow back. How long will it take? Weeks? Months? What do you have to eat to help the skin of your ass grow? Mackerel?

Do they want me to push a dump past open flesh? No way. How many days and weeks can I hold it in? And if I do manage to hold it in for a long time, the crap will get really big and harden and hurt even worse when it has to pass. I'll ask. They'll have to give me something to cause constipation so the wound can heal. I push my SOS button.

Waiting. While I wait I look through the other shots Robin took. Not one makes the wound look any less gruesome. What is that beside the wound? All sorts of red pimples. What the hell is that? I feel around both ass cheeks with my fingertips. I can feel the bumps. I didn't notice them before. My sense of touch is stunted compared to my sense of sight. I need to improve my sense of touch, this is no good. Where did these pimples come from? Allergies? Am I allergic to butt operations? I look at the photos again. Ah, now I know. It's razor burn. They shave you before an operation. Obviously not too daintily. Chop-chop, run the blade across. The only thing that matters is to get the hair off as quickly as possible. Probably without water or shaving cream. Just run the blade over, dry, to rip the hair out.

They're even more unceremonious about shaving than I am on my own. I used to not shave at all. I thought there were better ways to fritter away the time in the bathroom. And I found better ways. Until I met Kanell. He's from Africa. Ethiopia to be precise. One Saturday he stopped at the fruit-and-vegetable stand where I work to earn a little spending money. I set the stand up at four in the morning and sell produce until afternoon. My boss, the farmer who owns the stand, is a racist. Which is hilarious. Because he thinks he needs to stock exotic fruits and vegetables. A gap in the market. But who besides people from Africa, India, South America, or China knows how to prepare dishes with pomelos, sunchokes, and taro root?

So my boss rants all day long about foreigners, about what an insult it is that they want to shop at his stand, and about their accents. This despite the fact that he's attracting them because of what he's selling. Kanell didn't understand the farmer's question: "That it?"

He had to ask the farmer what he meant. The farmer was so patronizing in his explanation that I slipped away from the stand afterward to apologize.

I ran along the rows of stalls looking for him. Finally, I was standing behind him. I tapped him on the shoulder and he turned around. All out of breath, I said: "Hi. I'm sorry. I just wanted to say I was ashamed of the way my boss acted."

"I could tell."

"Good."

We laughed together.

Then I got nervous and couldn't think of anything better to say than: "I'm going back to the stand."

"Are you shaved?"

"What?"

"I asked whether you were shaved."

"No, why do you ask?"

"Because I'd love to shave you sometime. At my place."

"When?"

"Right after work. Whenever the market closes."

He writes his address down for me, folds the piece of paper up small, and pushes it into my dirty palm like a little present. This definitely qualifies as one of my most impulsive dates ever. I shove the note into the chest pocket of my green apron and walk proudly back to the racist's stand.

I don't want to think too much over the next few hours about what to expect at his apartment. Otherwise I'll get too anxious and might not even go. That would be a shame.

When I'm done for the day I shove my under-the-table wages in my pocket and head for the jotted-down address. I ring the bell labeled *Kanell*. Apparently it's his last name. Or perhaps he's got such a complicated name that, like some soccer players, he's just picked out a pseudonym that stupid

Europeans can pronounce. He buzzes the door open and calls down the staircase: "Second floor."

I step inside the entryway and the door closes hard behind me. It practically hits me and a cold breeze rustles my hair. The mechanical arm that closes the door is set too tight. There's a screw someplace in it that you can loosen so the door closes more elegantly. My father taught me that. If I start coming here often, I'll bring a screwdriver sometime and fix it.

I hike up my skirt and wriggle my hand into my underwear. I stick my middle finger deep into my pussy and leave it in the warmth for a moment before taking it back out. I open my mouth and stick my finger all the way in. I close my lips around my finger and pull it out slowly. I lick and suck as hard as I can in order to get as much of the taste of the slime on my tongue as possible.

There's no way I can spread my legs for some guy—to get thoroughly eaten out, for instance—without knowing myself how everything looks, smells, and tastes down there.

In our bathroom are all kinds of useful mirrors that help me look at my own pussy from below. A woman looking down over her stomach at her pussy from above sees it from a completely different perspective than a man with his head hung between her legs in bed.

A woman sees just a tuft of hair sticking up and two bumps hinting at the outer labia.

A man sees a gaping, hungry mouth with knots of flesh all over it. I want to see everything on me the same way a man sees it; they see more of a woman than she does herself because everything down there is oddly hidden, just out of view. In the same way I want to be the first to know how my slime looks, smells, and tastes. And not just lie there and hope everything comes out alright.

Whenever I go to the bathroom I dip my finger into my pussy before I piss and do the same test. I dig around, scoop out as much slime as possible, and sniff it. For the most part it smells good—as long as I haven't eaten a lot of garlic or Indian food.

The consistency varies a lot. Sometimes it's like cottage cheese, other times like olive oil, depending on how long it's been since I washed. And that depends on who I want to have sex with. Lots of guys prefer cottage cheese. You wouldn't think so. But it's true. I always ask in advance.

Then I suck it all off my finger and slurp it around in my mouth like a gourmand. Most of the time it tastes good. Except once in a while when the slime has a sour aftertaste. I haven't figured out what causes that yet, but I will.

The test has to be conducted every time I go to the bathroom because I often run into the dilemma—or unexpected pleasure—of spontaneous sex. Even in those situations I want to be up-to-date on my pussy's slime production. Helen leaves nothing to chance. Only when I know exactly what's going on with my beloved, precious slime can a man slurp it up with his tongue.

I've done the taste test and am happy. I'm ready to be looked at and tasted. The smegma has a bit of age to it, a truffle flavor, and that makes guys hot. Usually.

I climb the stairs. Not slowly, as if I do this all the time. No games. By walking up quickly, I show him how excited and curious I am. At the door he takes my hands in his and kisses me on the forehead. He leads me into the living room. It's very warm. The radiator is boiling away. Someone could comfortably hang out naked here for a good, long time. It's dark. The blinds are down. There's just a little table lamp with a twenty-five-watt bulb. It illuminates a bowl of steaming water on the floor. Next to that is a folded washcloth and an old-fashioned men's razor and a can of shaving cream. The entire couch is covered with big towels.

He quickly undresses me. The skirt is the only thing that gives him trouble—complicated clasp. Lifting it up isn't good enough for him. It's all got to go, the clothing. I help him. Then he lays me down at an angle on the couch. My head in the back corner, my butt on the front edge. I put a foot up on the arm to brace myself, so I'm lying there as if I'm at the gynecologist—Dr. Broekert position.

He undresses completely in front of me. I hadn't expected that. I thought I'd get undressed and he'd stay clothed. All the better. His nipples are hard and he has a partial erection. He has a very thin cock with an acorn-like tip, and it dangles to the left. That is, to my left.

He has a loaf of bread tattooed on his chest. The shape is more like a round sourdough than a loaf of rye or multi-grain bread. Gradually my breathing calms down. I get used to unusual situations quickly. I fold my arms behind my head and watch him. He's readying everything and seems pleased. Looks like there's nothing for me to do except lie back. We'll see.

He leaves the room and returns with a miner's lamp on his head. I have to laugh and tell him he looks like a Cyclops. We've just been reading about them in school. He laughs, too.

He puts a pillow on the floor and kneels on it, saying he doesn't want to get calluses on his knees. Then he dunks both hands into the hot water and rubs it onto my legs. Aha. He starts all the way down at my ankles, moving upward.

Then he sprays shaving cream into his hand and spreads it on my legs. He dunks the razor in the hot water and tracks it down the entire length of the leg. Where he's run the blade, the foam is gone. He makes one straight line after another. Like a lawnmower. After each razor run, he shakes the blade clean in the water. Hairs and foam are swimming on the surface. Fairly quickly, both legs are naked. He says I should have my armpits done the same way. Crap.

I was already looking forward to having my pussy shaved. If he's even planning to do that.

He wets both pits with water and sprays in the shaving cream. He has a harder time under the arms because the hair is longer. He has to go over some of the same spots several times to get it all off. My armpits are also very deep, so he has to pull the skin tight in various directions in order to be able to shave across flat surfaces. He throws a circle of light on my skin with his miner's light. When he gets close—to get a better view—the circle tightens and the light intensifies. When he pulls back, the lamp throws dim light on a wide area. The circle of light always illuminates the exact spot where he's looking at any moment. And the intensity of the light tells how carefully he's looking at the spot. I see the light fall frequently on my tits. More often on the right one, the one with the snake-tongue nipple. My face seems to hold little interest. Once everything is smooth, he ladles water from the bowl into my armpits to rinse away the shaving cream. Then he dries me off. And I dab myself with a towel, too. We smile at each other.

"And now," I say, patting my hair-covered pussy.

"Hmm."

He wets both hands and dampens the whole area. From my bellybutton down, left and right along my thighs, and then on down between my labia to my butthole and on to the top of my ass crack. He looks closely at the cauliflower. A shaving obstacle course. Then he sprays shaving cream on all the dampened areas. It tingles on the labia. Zhhhh. He massages the foam into the skin a little and reaches for his razor. He starts on the thighs. The pubic hair growing down my legs is shaved away. He puts the blade just below my bellybutton and stops. He leans back to get an overview of the area and a crease appears on his brow.

He says: "I like that the hair grows up that far. There I'm going to leave everything. I'll take a little off the sides so we'll have a long, dark stripe down to the split. Then from there all the way back, everything is coming off." He doesn't look me in the eyes, but talks instead to my pussy.

It answers: "Understood."

On the sides he mows the lawn down to a stripe. He tapers the stripe right to the point where the tops of the lady-fingers rise. Now he's on to the labia. Finally. Finally. He puts his head between my legs. That's the best way he can light up my pussy with his lamp. It must look like a hairy lantern. Glowing red inside. He carefully shaves my lady-fingers. Then he has to spread them because he wants to work on the inside edges, too. Again and again he makes his way through all the crevices. Until there's no foam to be seen anywhere. I want him to fuck me. Which he obviously will after the shaving. Have a little patience, Helen. He says I should spread my legs wider but bring my knees up closer to my body so he can get at my ass. He asks whether the bulges on my butt hurt.

"No, no, that's just hemorrhoids that have worked their way out. If you're gentle, I think you can shave right over them."

There's much less hair in back. He runs the razor up and down my butt crack a few times and once around the anus in a circle. Done. Once again I'm drizzled with what is now no longer hot water from the bowl. The shaving of my crack made my pussy produce a lot of slime. Now it mixes with the water and is dabbed dry by Kanell. But it oozes more immediately.

"Do you want to fuck me now?"

"No, you're too young for me."

Stay cool, Helen. Otherwise that nice feeling down below will disappear.

"Too bad. Do you mind if I fuck myself here then? Or do I have to wait until I get home to come?"

"Please go ahead. You are very welcome to do it here."

"Give me the razor."

I hold the blade end and shove the handle into my wet pussy. The handle's not as cold as I expected. Kanell's hands have warmed it up.

With rhythmic motions I let the handle glide in and out. It feels like the finger of a fourteen-year-old. Like Hansel's finger of bone. I rub the handle hard between my labia, back and forth. Harder. It's the same motion as cutting bread. Hard bread. Forward, back. Forward, back. Sawing. Sawing. Deeper.

Kanell watches me.

"Can you put the lamp on my head? I want to light myself up."

He stretches the elastic headband around my head and adjusts the lamp so it's exactly in the middle of my forehead. I look at my pussy and thereby light it up. Kanell walks out of the room. Ooh la la, shaving's got me hot. I lay the razor on my stomach and stroke my smooth-shaven, naked labia with both hands. Dear nonexistent God are they soft. Soft like kid leather, soft like avocado pits. So soft that I can barely even feel them with my fingers. I rub them faster. And come.

And now? I'm sweaty and out of breath. It's so hot in here. Where is Kanell? I get dressed. It's even warmer. He comes in.

I ask: "Do you want to do this again?"

"Love to."

"When?"

"Every Saturday after work."

"Good. That'll give me a week to grow the hair back for you each time. I'll give it my all. See you then."

That was the first time I shaved. Or rather, that I was shaved. Anyway: my first shave. Since then we see each other almost every week. Once in a while he doesn't buzz me in. Or he's not home. Then I have to run around for two weeks with stubble. I hate it. Either totally shaved or hairy. It always starts to itch worse and worse. So I have to do it if he doesn't. But I never do it anywhere near as well as he does. Not as slowly and not as affectionately.

Shaving myself is stupid—I'm spoiled in that regard now. I'm used to being shaved. I think that if men want shaved women, they should take over the shaving. Don't saddle the women with all the work. In the absence of men, women wouldn't care at all how hairy they were. The best arrangement I can imagine would be for men and women to shave each other in whatever way they find most pleasing. That way each would have the exact hairstyle that got their partner the hottest. Better than just hoping for the best from the other person or trying to explain it. That's nothing but trouble.

For me it's all about just getting it done. I shave myself fast, zigzagging all over the place, and rip myself to shreds. I'm usually bleeding afterward, and the open razor-burn bumps gets infected. Whenever Kanell sees that, he scolds me for treating myself that way. He can't stand it. But even I'm not as careless as the person who shaved me before the operation on my ass.

A nurse walks in. Unfortunately, it's not Robin. Oh well. I can ask her, too.

"What happens if I need to have a bowel movement?"

That's what they call it. I can break out that phrase, too, if I feel like it. Depending on who I'm talking to.

She explains that as far as the doctors are concerned, it's desirable that you take a crap as soon as possible. So no log jam develops. She says it's better for the wound to heal with regular bowel movements so that everything grows back together properly and is able to stretch normally. They must be out of their minds. She says Dr. Notz will be right in to explain everything. She walks out. While I'm waiting for Notz, I think about all the things that can cause constipation. So many things come to mind. Notz comes in. I greet him and look him right in the eyes. I always do that when I'm trying to intimidate someone. It occurs to me what long, full eyelashes he has. I can't believe it—why didn't I notice that before? Maybe I was too distracted by the pain. The longer I look at him, the longer and fuller his lashes become. He's telling me, I think, important things about my bowel movements, my diet, and my recovery. But I'm not listening. I'm counting his eyelashes. And making noises every now and again that are supposed to make it seem as if I'm listening closely. Uh-huh.

Eyelashes like that I call eye-mustaches. I can't stand it when men have beautiful lashes. Even on women it bugs me a little. Eyelashes are a constant theme in my life. I always pay attention to them. How long they are, how thick, what color they are, whether they're dyed, done up with mascara or with a lash curler, or both, whether they're stuck together with sleepy seeds. A lot are light at the ends and darker at the base so they look much shorter than they really are. If you were to put mascara on them, they'd suddenly look twice as long. Me, I had no lashes at all for many years of my childhood. But I know that before that I used to get lots of compliments on my long lashes.

One day a woman asked my mom if it didn't bother her that her six-year-old daughter had fuller lashes than she herself did, even though she used mascara and a lash curler. Mom always told me there was an old Gypsy saying: if you get too many compliments about one particular thing, that thing will eventually disappear. That was always her explanation, too, whenever I asked why I no longer had any lashes. I have a lingering mental image, though: In the middle of the night I wake up and mom is sitting on the side of my bed where she usually sits to read me stories. She's holding my head still, and I feel cold metal along the edge of my eyelids. Snip. On both eyes. And mom's voice says, "It's only a dream, my child."

With my fingertips I'd always touch the stubs of the lashes. If mom's Gypsy story were true, the lashes would have fallen out completely. But I can't really pin it on mom, either, because I often blur the distinctions between reality, lies, and dreams. These days in particular I can't keep things straight because of all the years I took drugs. The wildest party I ever had happened when my friend Corinna realized Michael, my drug-dealer boyfriend at the time, had forgotten his stash of drugs at her house. There was no occasion for a party. It's just what you say you're doing when you take drugs. Partying.

Michael kept all his blotters and pills and packets of speed and coke in a fake soda can. It looked just like a normal can of cola, but you could screw the top off.

Michael always tried to stuff enough drugs into it so it weighed exactly as much as a real can of cola would.

Corinna said: "Check it out, Helen—Michael's can. He wouldn't mind, would he?"

She grinned at me, wrinkling her nose in the process. That always means she's genuinely excited.

We blew off school, bought some red wine at a kiosk, and left a message for Michael on his answering machine: "If you're looking for cola, we found a whole case in Corinna's room. You won't get pissed if we start drinking without you, will you?"

We were big on using badly coded language over the phone. When you're taking drugs you get paranoid and confuse yourself with Scarface. You think you're being listened to and there's about to be a raid, arrests, and a court proceeding during which the judge will say, "So, Helen Memel, what do the words 'laundry detergent,' 'pizza,' and 'painting' really mean? At no point during this time were you doing laundry, eating pizza, or painting. We didn't just tap your phone; you were also under surveillance."

Then began our race against time. The idea was to take as many drugs as possible before the first one took effect and before Michael showed up. Anything we didn't slurp down we'd have to give back. At nine in the morning we started taking two pills at a time, washing them down with wine. It didn't seem right to snort speed and coke so early in the morning, so we made minigrenades out of toilet paper.

Half a packet for each us—which is half a gram—poured onto a little piece of toilet paper, skillfully wrapped up, and gulped down with lots of wine. Maybe there was less than a gram per packet—Michael was a good businessman and he messed with everyone a little on the amounts. So he could earn more. One time I weighed something that was supposed to be a gram. Not even close. But people can't exactly register a complaint with the police. That's just the way it is on the black market. No consumer protection.

Anyway, these paper grenades are very tough to get down. It takes practice. If it doesn't get washed down your throat right away, the minigrenade opens up and the bitter powder sticks to your mouth and gums. You definitely don't want that.

I guess everything started to kick in. I can only remember the highlights. Corinna and I laughed the whole time and made up stories set in a fantasy land. At some point Michael came by to pick up his can and cursed us out. We giggled. He said if all the stuff we'd ingested didn't kill us, we would have to pay him back. We just laughed.

Later we puked. First Corinna, then me from the sound and smell of hers. In a big, white bucket. The puke looked like blood because of the red wine. But it took us a long time to figure out why it looked like that. And then we realized there were undigested pills floating around. This seemed like a terrible waste to us.

I said: "Half and half?"

Corinna said: "Okay, you first."

And so for the first time in my life I drank someone else's puke. Mixed with my own. In big gulps. Taking turns. Until the bucket was empty.

A lot of brain cells die on days like that. And this, along with other similar parties, definitely took a toll on my memory. There's another memory that I've never been sure is even a memory. I come home one day from elementary school and call out hello. Nobody answers. So I think nobody's home.

Then I go into the kitchen and lying there on the floor are my mom and my brother. Hand in hand. They're asleep. My brother's head is resting on his Winnie the Pooh pillow and mom's is on a folded-up, light-green dish towel.

The oven door is open. It smells like gas. What to do? I saw a movie once where somebody struck a match and the whole house blew up. So, nice and slow, I carefully creep over to the oven—there are people sleeping here—and turn off the gas. Then I open the windows and call the fire department. I can't think of the number for the hospital in order to get an ambulance. Oh, both are on the way . . . yes, they're still sleeping . . . I can ride with them. Two ambulances. A whole crew. Flashing blue lights. Sirens. They have their stomachs pumped at the hospital and dad comes directly from work.

Nobody in the family has ever spoken about it. At least not with me. That's why I'm not sure whether maybe I dreamed it or made it up and have just convinced myself it's true over the years. It's possible.

Mom trained me to be a good liar. To such a degree that I believe most of my own lies. Sometimes it can be fun.

Other times it can be maddening, as in this case. I guess I could just ask mom.

"Mom, did you used to cut off my eyelashes out of jealousy? And another thing: Did you try to kill yourself along with my brother? And: Why didn't you want to take me with you?"

I never find the right moment.

At some stage my eyelashes grew back and I always curled them and used mascara to make the best out of them —and to piss off my mother in case that memory is a genuine memory. Top and bottom, I want my real lashes to look like plastic false eyelashes from the sixties. I mix cheap and expensive mascara to make the ultimate lashes. The best way is to use the end of the brush, where the mascara accumulates, and just glob it onto the lashes. The goal is for people half a mile away to think: "Wow, she's a walking set of lashes."

Mascara is always advertised as not being sticky, and the brush is always supposed to keep the lashes separate so there are no clumps. But for me those are reasons *not* to buy a mascara. When my relatives and neighbors figured out that I never remove the mascara and just put more on every day, a panic broke out.

"If you don't remove the mascara from your lashes, they never get any light or air—and then they'll fall out."

I thought: It couldn't be any worse than it used to be. And I thought up cool tricks to avoid water ever getting on my lashes. After putting so much money and effort into my lashes, I can't just let them get ruined in the shower. And besides, when months' worth of mascara slowly dissolves in hot water and runs into your eyes, it burns. You definitely don't want that. So I shower in stages. First I wash my hair and wrap it in a towel so the water can't get into my eyes. Then I do the rest of my body from the neck down. For a while I missed my neck and black, greasy smudges would accumulate in the three indentations at the base of it.

When that happens, if you rub your neck, dark, sticky little rolls form that smell like pus. So you either have to wash from the face down or you have to rub these rolls off your neck regularly. But the important thing is that your face never comes in contact with water. I haven't put my head underwater for years—not in the bathtub or in the school swimming pool. I have to climb into the pool by the stairs like a granny, and I can only swim the breaststroke because your face, or parts of it, go under water with any other stroke. If someone tries to dunk me, I turn into a fury and scream and beg and explain that it would ruin my lashes. That's worked so far.

For years I haven't seen water from below the surface. Obviously that means I never wash my face either. I think it's overrated anyway. When you take your makeup off with makeup remover and cotton balls you're kind of washing your face. Just keep your distance from the eyelashes. That's the way I've been doing it for years. Only one or two lashes have gotten stuck in the curler. And they grew back. So I've proved that your lashes don't all fall out if you don't remove your mascara every night.

My ex-boyfriend Matt watched me curl my lashes once and asked me whether a row of eyelashes was the same length as the inner pussy lips.

"Yeah. Approximately."

"And you have two of these curlers?"

"Yep."

A gold one and a silver one.

He laid me down on the bed. Spread my legs. Pushed aside the ladyfingers and gently clamped my dewlaps with the eyelash curlers. That way he could hold the inner labia away from the hole and look deep inside. A bit like when they force Malcolm McDowell's eyes open in *A Clockwork Orange*. He asked me to hold the curlers and pull them as far apart as felt good. Matt wanted to fuck me immediately and cum on my stretched lips. But first he wanted to take a picture so I could see how pretty my pussy looked all stretched apart. We clapped our hands with joy. Well, he did. My hands were busy.

When you stretch these crinkly flaps of skin all the way out, the total surface is as big as a postcard. At some point Matt drifted out of my life, but his good idea stayed with me.

I like the feeling I get from stretching my lips with the lash curlers until they look from my perspective like bat wings. Actually, I wonder if that's why they're so big and peek out from the ladyfingers? No way. I'm sure they were always so big and long and frayed grayish pink along the edges. All of this goes through my head as I'm ignoring Dr. Notz. Now he wants to leave.

But here comes Helen with the photos of her ass.

He needs to tell me which side is up. I can't make out an asshole anywhere. No matter which way I turn the camera.

I look at him. He looks at the photos and quickly away again. He's disgusted by the results of his own surgical work. No wonder he didn't want to tell me beforehand what he had in mind.

"At least tell me which way I need to hold it to see what it looks like down there."

"I can't tell. In my opinion the photo was taken too close up. I can't tell which way it goes, either."

He sounds angry. Is he crazy? He's the one who did this to me. I didn't mess around with his ass. As far as I'm concerned, I'm the victim and he's the culprit.

He keeps glancing at the photo and then looking immediately away again. Hopefully he's able to keep his eyes on wounds for a bit longer when he's in the operating room. What a sissy. Or does he enter another world in the operating room? Looks at everything closely in there and just can't stand to be confronted with it afterward?

Like somebody who always goes to a brothel and does the wildest, most intimate, filthy things with the same hooker, but who, if he runs into her on the street, looks away and would never say hello.

He didn't greet my asshole very nicely.

He doesn't want to see it again.

I see panic in his eyes: Help! My little operating room asshole can speak, ask questions. It's even taken photos of itself.

There's no point. He just doesn't know how to communicate with the people attached to the asses he operates on.

"Thanks a lot, Mr. Notz." That's supposed to signal that he should leave. I dropped his professional title. That does the trick. He walks out.

After the operation and the explanation by the esteemed Dr. Notz, I should now be crapping merrily. One sentence in his long-winded talk caught my attention: I will be discharged from the hospital only after a successful bowel movement with no bleeding. That is the indicator that the operation's been a success and that everything's healing properly.

From this point on, people who have never been introduced to me before come in every few minutes and ask whether I've had a bowel movement. Noooo, not yet! The fear of the pain is insurmountable. If I were to press a log of crap past that wound, my God, what would happen? It would rip me open.

Since the operation I've had only granola and whole-grain bread. They tell me my granola shouldn't sit in the milk too long before being consumed. It should make it into the stomach and intestines in a fairly dry state. That way it will absorb fluid in the body and swell, pushing against the intestinal walls from the inside and thus signaling that it wants out.

The urge to crap should be greatly heightened that way. They're chucking bombs in the top but down below I'm all cinched up with fear. I'm not going to crap for days. I'll just do as my mother does—wait for everything to disintegrate inside.

Can you eat pizza while you're waiting to take a crap? I don't ask anybody; I decide that it's important for rectal healing to eat things you like. I call my favorite pizza delivery service, Marinara. I know the number by heart. It's easy to remember, like those phone-sex lines. I'm really excited, but I don't let it show. I try to sound as belligerent as possible: "One mushroom pizza. Two beers. Saint Mary's Hospital, room 218. The name is Memel. And make it quick. It better not be cold when it gets here. Just go to the front desk and they'll call me."

I hang up as quick as I can.

There's an urban legend that made the rounds a while ago; I think a lot about it. Two girls order a pizza. They wait and wait but the pizza never comes. They call the delivery service a few times and complain. Eventually the pizza shows up.

It looks a little funny and tastes odd. By coincidence, one of the girls is the daughter of a food inspector, and instead of munching the rest they put it in a bag and take it to dad.

They all think maybe the pizza's gone bad or something. Instead it comes out in the lab analysis that there are five different people's sperm on the pizza. This is how I picture it getting there: The guys at the delivery service are annoyed by the phone calls. Since the complaints are being made by girls, the delivery guys have rape fantasies. The usual. They talk about it, come up with a plan, and all whip out their cocks to jerk off on a pizza. The pizza baker sees all the other guys' cocks. And not just in their normal state. Fully erect. Being jerked off and coming. That's why I'm envious of men. I'd like to see the pussies of my friends and schoolmates. And the cocks of my friends and schoolmates. Especially when they're all coming. But you hardly ever have the chance. And I don't dare ask.

I only get to see the cocks of men I'm fucking and the pussies of women I pay.

I want to see more in life.

That's why I love to break into the public pool and go drunken skinny-dipping after a night out clubbing.

The whole trespassing thing is a little problematic. But at least you get to see a few cocks and pussies.

Anyway. I'm always extra mean whenever I order pizza. And I complain even when it doesn't take long. I'd love to eat a pizza with sperm from five different guys on it.

It would be like having sex with five strange men at the same time. Okay, maybe not exactly sex. But it would be like having five strange men blow their loads in my mouth at the same time. That would be something for the memory vault, right? To be able to say you'd done that: well done.

I can't even walk. So there's no way I can pick up the pizza. Shit. Now I'm leaking. No way. I'll have to ask someone to pick it up for me. There's no way the receptionist is going to walk around passing out pizzas. Robin will have to do it. The emergency buzzer. Is that wrong? Oh, well.

A different nurse comes in. His name tag says Peter. It makes me smile. I like the name Peter. I was with one once. I called him Piss Peter. He was really good at going down on me. He would do it for hours. He had quite a unique technique.

He would clamp the dewlaps between his teeth and his tongue and then rub his tongue over them. Back and forth. Or with his tongue flattened out and a lot of spit he'd lick from my asshole up to my snail tail and back down. Pressing hard against all the folds.

Both techniques were very good. I usually came multiple times. Once so hard that I pissed in his face. He was mad because he thought I had done it on purpose. It was a little humiliating—the way he was kneeling there and then that happened.

I patted him dry and apologized. I thought he should be proud. Nobody else had ever accomplished that. To make me come so hard that I lose control of my bladder. And I wasn't drunk or anything.

After a while he realized how impressive it was. I learned that day from Piss Peter that it burns when you get piss in your eye. How else could I have ever found that out?

"Where's Robin?"

"Shift change. I'm the night shift."

Is it already that late? Do the days in a hospital go by that fast? Apparently. I'm losing my mind. Fine. It's not so bad here, Helen. Time flies when you amuse yourself with your own thoughts.

"How can I help you?"

"I wanted to ask Robin a favor. I'm a little uncomfortable asking you. We don't know each other."

"What was the favor?"

"I ordered a pizza. It's going to be delivered downstairs soon and I can't go get it. I need someone who can walk and is willing to bring it up here."

Maybe a nurse like this isn't interested in real nourishment, and this plan will fall flat.

"Aren't you supposed to eat high-fiber foods after the operation? Granola, whole-grain breads?"

Shit.

"Yes. I am. Doesn't pizza have any fiber?"

Super idea. Play dumb.

"No. It's actually counterproductive."

Counterproductive—against production. Everybody here thinks only about bowel movements. It's my choice.

"But it's also important to eat things your stomach is accustomed to. Sudden changes in diet aren't good, either, for encouraging bowel movement. Please."

The phone rings.

I answer.

"Is the pizza here?"

I hold the phone to the side and smile at Peter, eyebrows raised in question marks.

"I'll go get it. We'll see what happens," he says, smiling handsomely as he leaves.

"Nurse Peter will come get it. Don't give it to anyone else. Thanks."

I'm lucking out with these male nurses. They're much nicer than the female ones.

I lie back and wait for Peter.

It's dark outside. I can see myself reflected in the window. The bed is very high so the nurses don't hurt their backs maneuvering the patients. The glass goes the entire length of the wall from right to left and from the ceiling down to the radiator. When it's dark outside and light inside it functions like a giant mirror. I didn't need the camera at all, eh? I turn my ass to the window and crane my head as best I can. It's all blurry. Of course. It's double-pane glass. It reflects two images, slightly staggered. Good to have the camera after all. When it's dark out I can lie with my ass to the door and see who's entering the room without turning around. Cool. But can everybody outside see me now? Oh, who cares. They know it's a hospital. It's impossible not to recognize it. At worst they'll think it's a poor little crazy girl who, out of her head on medication, left her bare ass facing the window—and they'll feel sorry for me. That works for me.

Here in the hospital I'm becoming sort of a nudist. I'm not usually like that. Well, when it comes to things pussy-related I guess I am. But not when it comes to my ass.

I just lie here and, because any motion hurts my ass so bad, I don't even bother to cover myself. Anyone who comes in sees my gaping flesh wound and a bit of my peach. You get used to it quickly. Nothing is embarrassing any-more. I'm an ass patient. Anyone can see that, and I be-have accordingly.

The reason I have such a healthy attitude about my pussy while I'm normally so uptight about my ass is that the way my mother raised me made it difficult for me to crap. When I was a little girl she told me all the time that she never went to the bathroom. And never farted. She held everything inside until it disintegrated. No wonder I had trouble.

As a result of being told all of this, I get totally ashamed if someone hears or smells me going to the bathroom. In public toilets, even if I'm just pissing and a fart escapes when I loosen the muscles down there, I'll do anything to avoid the person in the next stall being able to put a face to the noise. I'm the same way with the smell of my crap. When people are coming and going in the stalls around me and I've stunk the place up, I'll wait in my stall until there are no more witnesses around. Only then will I come out.

As if crapping is a crime. My schoolmates always laugh at me for my exaggerated sense of shame.

I also don't like to get dressed in my room at home. There are posters everywhere of my favorite bands. They're always looking right into the camera for the photos, so it feels as if they are following my every move with their eyes. So if I'm changing in my room and they could get a peek at my pussy or tits, I hide behind my couch. Though around real boys and men I don't care.

Someone knocks. Peter walks in. He places the pizza on the metal nightstand and puts the two bottles of beer down—a little too loudly—next to it. It all just barely fits.

He looks me in the eye the whole time. I stare back. I'm good at that. I think he likes taking care of someone roughly the same age as he is. It's nice for him.

"You want one of the beers?"

"That's nice of you, but I'm working. If I walk around here with beer breath there'll be hell to pay."

I hate being told no. I should have been able to figure out that he's not allowed to drink on the job. Embarrassing. This is a hospital, Helen, not a bordello.

His gaze starts to wander. Is he looking out the window? Past me? Wait, no, he must be looking at my peach reflected in the window. His nightshift is starting off well. I like Peter.

"Okay, thanks. I guess I'll eat."

He leaves. I open up the pizza box and look at it. I wonder how I'll be able to eat it without any utensils. The Marinara guys haven't even cut the crust with a pizza roller. Should I rip bites out of it like an animal? Suddenly Peter walks back in. With silverware. And walks back out grinning. And then comes in again. What now? In his hand is a plastic baggie with a piece of tape on it. There's something written on the tape.

"It says here I'm supposed to give this to you. Something to do with the operation. Do you know anything about it? Did they find something on you and need to return it?"

"I wanted to see the wedge of skin after they cut it out of me. I couldn't let something be cut out of me while I was unconscious and then not see it before it was tossed in the garbage."

"Speaking of garbage, it's my job to ensure this baggie and its contents are properly disposed of in the special medical-waste bin."

He takes his duties very seriously. He speaks in such a highbrow manner about them. He could have just said he had to make sure the stuff got thrown out instead of "properly disposed of." It would make him seem more human and less like a robot repeating orders. He hands me the baggie but doesn't leave. But I'm only going to open it when I'm alone. I hold the baggie in my hands and stare at Peter until he finally leaves. My pizza is getting cold. But this is more important—and besides, I've heard real gourmets don't eat things really hot because it masks the flavors. Really hot soup tastes like nothing at all. It must be true of pizza, too. If you make something poorly, just serve it as hot as possible and nobody will notice it tastes bad because they'll all have charred their taste buds. It's true of the other extreme, too: cold. You drink nasty drinks—like tequila—as cold as possible so you can get them down.

The baggie is see-through, zipped shut. A little slide is all it takes to open it. Inside is another bag, smaller and white instead of see-through. I can feel the cut-out piece inside it. No more packaging. If I just pull it out it'll make a mess here in the bed. I rip off the top of the pizza box. It's easy. It's perforated along the edge, probably for just such a situation. When you need something to put a bloody piece of flesh on. I put the cardboard box top in my lap beneath the baggie. Do I need rubber gloves to pull this thing out? No. It's from my own body. So I can't catch anything, no matter how bloody it is. I touch what used to surround this clump of flesh—my gaping wound—all day long without gloves. Okay. So out it comes. It feels like liver or something else from the butcher shop. I lay out all the pieces on the card-board. I'm disappointed. Lots of little pieces. No wedge. Notz's description made it sound as if it would be a thin, oblong piece of flesh that would look like the venison filets mom makes when we have guests in the fall and winter. Dark red and slick before being roasted, kind of shiny, like liver. But this here is goulash. Little pieces. Some pieces have yellow spots—the infection, no doubt—that look the way freezer burn does in commercials. They didn't cut it out in one motion, not all together in one single piece. Of course, I'm no dead deer, but a living girl. Perhaps it's better that they took care of it in small increments. And paid attention to the sphincter. Rather than carving out a magnificent anal filet just for the sake of a good presentation. Relax, Helen. Things are always different than you anticipate. At least you tried to picture something, imagined the smallest details, asked questions to try to verify things—and now you know more as a result. I learned that from dad. To try to figure things out so thoroughly it makes you puke. Anyway, I'm happy to have seen the pieces before they're cremated along with the other medical waste. I don't repack the pieces into the baggie. I just put the baggie on top of them and push it down so it sticks to them. I put the box top with the pieces of flesh and baggie on it on the metal nightstand. My fin-gers are covered with blood and goop. Wipe them on the bed? That would make a real mess. Not on my tree-top-angel outfit, either. Same mess. Hmm. Well. It is all stuff from my own body. Even if it's infected. I lick my fingers off one at a time. I'm always proud of myself when I come up with an idea like that. It's better than sitting helplessly in bed and hoping somebody happens by with wet wipes. Why should I be disgusted by my own blood and pus? I'm not squeamish about infections. When I pop pimples and get pus on my finger, I happily eat that. And when I squeeze a blackhead and the translucent little worm with the black head comes out, I wipe that up with a finger and then lick it off. When the sandman leaves puslike crumbs in the corners of my eyes, I eat them in the morning, too. And when I have scabs on a cut, I always pick off the top layer in order to eat it.

I eat my pizza by myself.

I don't like eating alone. It scares me. When you stick something in your mouth, you should be able to tell someone else what it tastes like. My ass begins to twitch. What have you learned, Helen? Don't suffer any more than necessary. Ring the emergency buzzer. Peter comes in and I tell him I need painkillers because the pain is starting up again. He looks confused and says there's nothing about overnight pain medication on the chart he's been given. With a big piece of pizza in my mouth I say, "There must be, Robin said all I had to do was ask and I'd get them."

This can't be happening. I finally ask before it gets bad and now I can't get any for the entire night? Help. Peter leaves to call the doctor at home. He says he doesn't have the authority to do anything that's not specifically listed on the chart. I'm feeling sick with fear. I was operated on today and I can't get any pain medication on the first night? I open both beers with the handle of the fork. I'm one of the few girls I know who can do that. Very practical. Hi ho, hi ho, it's off to work I go. I drink the beers down as fast as I can, one after the other. My ass is getting worse and worse, and my insides are cold from the beer.

Peter, Peter, Peter, hurry up. Bring me medication. I close my eyes. The pain is getting stronger and I'm beginning to cramp up. I know this drill. I cross my hands on my chest and I'm nothing more than my ass.

I hear him come in and, with my eyes still closed, ask whether I'll get something.

"What are you talking about," says a female voice.

I open my eyes and see a woman in a nurse's uniform but one that's a different color from all the others here. The others all wear light blue and she's in light green. Maybe she had a laundry mishap.

"Good evening. Please forgive me for disturbing you so late. The rounds took longer than usual today. I'm a candy striper."

What? She must have broken out of the psychiatric ward. I just look at her. She must be crazy, I think, and I'll leave her to believe what she wants. My ass hurts bad. And it's getting worse. That's the only thing I could possibly say to her. That would be a great conversation: "I'm a candy striper." "Yeah, and my ass hurts."

I watch her with tired, half-open eyes like a grandmother. It seems to me she talks very slowly—each word seems to echo.

"That means I'm a volunteer. I try to make things more comfortable for the people here in the hospital. We candy stripers"—there are others!—"run errands for patients, get them phone cards, pick up their mail, that sort of thing."

Very well.

"Can you get me painkillers?"

"No, we're not authorized to do that. We're not nurses. We just look like them." She snorts. It's supposed to be a laugh.

"Please leave me alone. I'm sorry, but I'm in pain and I'm waiting for a nurse and some medication. Normally I'm nicer. I'll call you if I need anything."

As she leaves, she asks, "Where would you call?"

Get out. I need peace and quiet.

I'm not going to be able to keep it together much longer. I take deep breaths. And blow them back out loudly. My hand wanders down to my pubic mound and I pull my knees up toward my chest. Although this position hurts, I stay in it. Into the pain with you, Helen. The other hand I put over my ass crack. This is bad. The kind of pain that makes you feel extremely lonely and scared. I think to myself, no patient should have to be in pain in a country as rich as this; I think, there's enough medicine for everyone here. I ring the buzzer. Peter comes running in. He apologizes that it's taken so long. He couldn't reach the doctor at first. He found out that the day shift had made a mistake. I was supposed to get an electronic device so I could self-administer pain medication. They were supposed to have the anesthesiologist attach one that would allow me just to click with my thumb to get doses of the medicine through the catheter in my arm. They forgot. Forgot? I'm at their mercy. Forgot. And now?

"You can have strong tablets upon request all night long. Here's the first one."

I pop it into my mouth and wash it down with the dregs of the beer. Peter clears away the pizza box. He's probably forgotten he's responsible for the medical waste. Hospital of the forgetful. My painkillers forgotten, my rectal goulash forgotten. We'll see what else gets forgotten. The half-eaten mushroom pizza sits on top covering everything. My goulash ends up in the normal trash. I like that. I don't say anything. He also throws out the beer bottles, very carefully so they don't bang against each other. Very delicate, Peter.

Because of the pain, my shoulder muscles are pulled all the way up to my ears, stretched taut like rubber bands. Now, after taking the pill, they begin to slowly relax and I can breathe more easily. I need to piss from the beer, but I can't get up. No worries. I fall asleep.

When I wake up it's still dark. I don't have a clock. Wait, my camera has a clock in it. I turn it on and take a picture of the room; when I view a shot, it always says when it was taken, right? 2:46 a.m. Too bad. I'd hoped the pill would allow me to sleep through the night. Did Peter leave more pills here?

I turn on the light. It's terribly bright and white. I'm dizzy. I guess these tablets they're giving me are pretty strong.

I'm having trouble thinking straight. My eyes adjust to the nightmarish light. Why did I bother with the clock in the camera? I have a mobile phone. You're funny sometimes, Helen. It must be the medication. I hope. I see a tablet in a little plastic cup on the nightstand. Down the hatch. I can do it without a drink. It tastes disgustingly chemical. It takes a long time before I have enough spit to swallow it. Gulp. And it's down. I turn off the light and try to go back to sleep. Can't. My bladder's full. Very full. At least it's my bladder bothering me and not my ass. There's a noise bothering me. It's a loud hissing. From outside, I think. Sounds like the exhaust pipe of the hospital's air-conditioning system. They must have moved it right outside my window while I was asleep. I refuse to go to the bathroom. You're going to have to fall asleep with a full bladder, Helen, or not at all. To block out the hiss I put the pillow on top of my head. Top ear blocked by the pillow, bottom ear by the mattress.

The hiss in my head is now as loud as the air conditioner outside. I press my eyelids together and try to force myself to sleep. Think about something else, Helen. But what?

I smell something.

I fear it's gas. I sniff and sniff again. It still smells like gas. A gas leak. I can almost hear it. Sssssssss. Just to be sure not to make a fool of myself, I wait a little while longer. I hold my breath. I count a few seconds and then take another deep breath. It's definitely gas. Turn on the light. I stand up. The motion hurts. But who cares. Better to have your ass hurt than to get blown sky high.

I go out into the hall and call.

"Hello? Is anyone there?"

Mom always forbid us to call out "hello." She thought it sounded as if you were talking down to handicapped people.

I'll make an exception. It's an emergency.

"Hello?"

It's silent in the hallway. Hospitals are creepy at night.

A nurse comes out of the nurses' station. Thankfully it's not a man. Where's Peter?

"Can you come check this out? It smells like gas in my room."

Her face becomes very serious. Good, she believes me.

We go into my room and sniff around. I can't smell it anymore. The strong gas smell. It's gone. No gas, no nothing. It's happened again.

"Oh, no, I guess it doesn't. My mistake." I exaggeratedly raise the corners of my mouth.

I'm hoping to make it look as if I was joking.

I don't pull it off very well. I can't believe I've fooled myself again. For the hundredth time. Approximately.

She looks at me full of disdain and leaves. She's right—it's nothing to joke about. But it wasn't meant to be one.

The worst gas incident so far—except for the real one—happened at home. One night when I was trying to fall asleep I was sure I smelled gas. The smell just kept getting stronger. Because I know gas is lighter than air—even though it's hard to believe—I thought I was well situated lying there in bed. It's not far off the floor.

I also know it takes a long time for all the rooms of a building to fill with gas and for the gas to slowly descend from the ceiling and spread out. I was sure my mom and brother were already dead. Whether the leak was in the basement or the kitchen, their rooms would be full by now.

I lay in bed a long time with my eyes nearly closed—because of lack of oxygen, I thought, though it turned out to be from sleepiness—thinking about what I should do.

I thought if I got out of bed I might cause a spark and it would be my fault if the apartment blew up and I died. The others were already dead—it wouldn't matter to them if the place exploded.

I decided to climb out of bed very slowly and inch my way outside on the floor.

The apartment was silent. If I made it out alive I would still have my father, who, luckily, didn't live in that deadly building. That's the one advantage to having divorced parents.

Lying on the floor I reached up for the handle of the front door and opened it. It took a long time to make it down the hall, snaking my way across the carpet. As soon as I was outside I took a few deep breaths. I'd made it.

I walked away from the building so I wouldn't be hit by any flying bricks if the place blew up.

I stood on the sidewalk in my nightgown, lit up by the only street lamp on our block, and looked at the tomb of my mother and brother.

There was a light on in the living room. I could see mom on the couch with a book in her hand. At first I thought she had suffocated and was frozen in that position. Rather improbable.

Then she turned a page. She was alive, and I realized I had fooled myself again.

I went back in and flopped down in bed. Real hard, to cause sparks.

There's no way for me to know whether I'm imagining it or not when I smell gas. It always smells strong. And it happens pretty often.

It's actually a pleasant smell.

Fear makes you tired. Painkillers, too. I lie down in the hospital bed and fall asleep.

I sleep through the rest of the night. Only two tablets. Not bad. I convince myself that's a small amount of pain medication. To be honest, yesterday evening I had pictured a more difficult night ahead. In a shotglass-sized plastic cup on the nightstand is a pill. Another one. Very generous, Peter. Pain medication, I assume. I slurp it down. Today I'll try to stand up. I also need to go to the bathroom. Bad. It doesn't smell good in here. It's not gas this time. It can only be my ass. What else?

I feel around in back and find it wet. Blood? I look at my fingers. Not red. A hint of light brown. I smell them. Definitely crap. How did that get there, inspector Helen?

From the container on the windowsill I pull out gauze bandages and wipe myself up. It's brown water that smells like crap. In the photo yesterday my butthole was wide open and I think everything must just be running out because the hole is still not tightly closed the way it normally would be. The seal isn't watertight. I christen the stuff coming out "ass piss" and I'm already used to it. I figure out a folding technique for the bandages: I hold my ass cheeks apart and shove my folded masterpiece up as close to the wound as possible so it stems the flow of ass piss. When I touch the wound itself with the bandages or my fingertips, it hurts bad. I gingerly let go of my ass cheeks. They hold the bandages in place. All set. Problem solved.

It really doesn't smell too good in this room. I'm afraid my ass is definitely air-incontinent. A constant flow of warm air is coming without warning out of my intestines. You can't even call them farts. My ass is just wide open. Farts have a beginning and an end. They noisily find their way out, sometimes with a lot of pressure. That's not the case here. It just billows out. And fills the room with all the smells that should stay inside me until I decide to let them out. It smells like warm pus mixed with diarrhea and something acidic that I can't seem to identify. Maybe it's from the medication.

Now when somebody enters the room they know as much about me as if under normal circumstances they had shoved their head up my ass and taken a big whiff.

I'm in a good mood because I slept so well, I think. The next problem: going to the bathroom. I lie on my stomach and drop my legs slowly toward the floor. It's a long way down. These tall beds. Bad. My feet touch the ground. I brace myself with my forearms and lift my upper body upright. I stand up. Ha! Turn around and slowly shuffle with tiny steps—otherwise it hurts my butt too much—what seems like a long way to the bathroom. Three yards. Plenty of time to think of something nice. The smell of this watery ass piss seems familiar to me.

When I know I'm going to have sex with someone who likes anal, I ask: with or without a chocolate dip? Which means: some guys like it when the tip of their cock has a little crap on it when they pull it out after butt fucking—the smell of the crap their cock's pulled out turns them on. Others want the tightness of the asshole without the filth. To each his own. For those who would rather have it clean, I ordered something from an online gay sex shop. It looks like a dildo with holes in the tip. It's made out of surgical steel. I don't know what that is, but it sounds good—and looks good.

First I unscrew my friendly showerhead so I can attach the threaded base of this device. It's handy that everything is standardized. Then it's time to clean the rectum. I smear the tip of the steel thing with Pjur lube. Then I work the thing past my cauliflower and shove it in as far as I can. At least that's the way I used to do it—the cauliflower's gone now. Should make it easier. Pushing it in turns me on—usually when something goes up my ass like that it's a cock. Is that Pavlovian conditioning?

The device is colder and harder than a cock. I turn on the shower full blast, but not too hot because I don't want to boil my innards. This is the best part of my internal cleansing. It feels like you're being pumped up like a balloon. We're more used to the feeling of being filled up from flatulence than from having water in our intestines. So you tend to picture gas, not water. Soon you feel like you're going to burst, like there are liters of water inside you. I get a strong urge to crap.

I turn the water off and crouch down as if I'm going to piss in the shower. I push all the water out of my intestines. It's like pissing out of your ass. Like having severe diarrhea. You need to take out the hair strainer and the tub stopper because a lot of crap comes out, in big and small chunks. I repeat this process three times until there are no more mini-chunks of crap visible. No cock, no matter how big or long, is going to unearth anything in my rectum now. I'm perfectly prepared for clean butt sex, like a blow-up doll.

If somebody does like a chocolate dip, I'll only do it if I've already had good sex with him a few times. It's a real sign of affection. Anal sex without cleaning my ass out in advance. It takes a lot of trust to let someone decorate his cock with my crap. If I haven't emptied my insides right before sex—either with the anal flushing device or on the toilet—there's crap ready to be found just a few centimeters inside the entrance. It doesn't get any more intimate than that as far as I'm concerned. Everything smells like my innards during sex like that, too. I have to smell my own innards the whole time. He only has to have stuck it in for a second and come in contact with the crap. Then when he pulls it back out and we try out another position, his cock functions like a fluttering crap-scented air freshener.

Right now, though, I can't imagine ever doing it again. Either thing. Ass cleansing or ass fucking. Which would be a shame.

I've made it. I've arrived in the bathroom. I don't need to pull my underwear down because I don't have any on. I just gather my tree-top angel outfit together on my stomach and tie it in a knot so it doesn't dangle into the toilet. I carefully try to sit down, but as I start to squat I realize it won't work. I can feel the wound straining. I'll have to stand upright and straddle the toilet bowl. That works. This is how French women piss, right? On the wall to my left is a grandma grab-bar to hold onto. Probably designed more to help lift yourself up if you've sat down and can't get back up. I'm misusing it to keep my balance while pissing standing up. I brace myself on the right against the plastic wall of the shower stall. I get most of the piss in the toilet. Am I supposed to take a crap like this? Can't possibly imagine that. Though I can't imagine taking a crap in any position. I'm not ready to try. Naturally, I don't wash my hands after pissing.

If I were able to sit down on the toilet seat I'd do what I usually do at home: read the labels of the various soaps and shampoos on the rim of the tub. Apparently mom has put a few things around the sink here for me. But I can't reach them right now. At home I know a lot of the label information by heart. My favorite is a bubble bath: "Toning and Invigorating." No idea what that's supposed to mean. Invigorating I understand, I guess. But toning? I've tried to picture mom toned. It's not a pretty picture. And ever since this word entered my vocabulary, I've been calling my brother Toning instead of Tony. He doesn't find it amusing. But I do.

Quickly—but slowly—back to bed.

It's going to take an extremely long time to get there. I never would have thought the butthole was so integral to the process of walking. During this turtle-speed walk I have plenty of time to think about all the things I want to do today. I'm sure my father and mother will visit. I'll get them back together. I also need to set up my avocado pits and fill the glasses with water. I'll have to find a hiding place for them or they'll be taken away. I've made it as far as the Jesus poster. I take it off the wall and carry it with me toward the bed. It'll fit perfectly between the metal nightstand and the wall, where no one can see it. Beautiful. An atheist hospital room. I crawl up onto my bed like a cripple and I've made it. What's this? There are drops of liquid on the floor. A long trail. From the bathroom to the bed, with a detour to the wall. It's drops of pee. I didn't wipe. Never do. But usually it goes into my underwear or whatever I'm wearing. Here I'm not wearing anything down below so it all drips onto the floor. Funny. There's no way I can go back and wipe it up—I can't walk that far again much less squat down to wipe something at floor level. It'll have to stay there. I count the drops I can see, as far as the bathroom door. Twelve. The sun streaming in the window reflects off drops nine and ten so they look like little circles cut out of aluminum foil or something else shiny. My father is a scientist and he taught me that some beams of light are broken and diffuse in a drop of liquid. That's why it looks as if light has been trapped inside a droplet. The rest of the light is reflected by the surface of the liquid. That's why it shines.

There's a knock at the door and someone in white medical clogs walks along the pee path. The socks are gleaming white. Nothing in our house ever stays white. Anything white takes on a different shade after the first washing. A dirty pink or grayish brown. More people walk in. The drops get all trampled. All these people have my pee on the bottoms of their shoes. That's my kind of humor. I imagine how all day long they'll be walking around their various stations and marking my territory for me. What are they doing here other than ruining my pee path?

Aha. It must be doctors and residents, or whatever you call them. They're doing rounds. Why is it called that anyway? They've already introduced themselves. Asked me questions. And I've been thinking about other things. I can continue now. The best spot for the avocados would be the windowsill. Because of the light. I'll just have to screen it off so that nobody standing in the room can see them.

I hear the sentence, "She'll be discharged once she has a successful bowel movement."

Of course. They're talking about me. The bowel movement lady. It's Notz. I hadn't noticed him among all the other doctors. Can I ask someone to fill the avocado glasses with water? I can't possibly go back and forth filling them all. Given the speed I'm walking right now, it could take days. I have glasses for the pits and another one for mineral water. Someone will have to use that one to fill the others, going back and forth between the windowsill and sink. Wait, I've got it. I can use the mineral water for the pits. The nurses always refill my glass. So I don't need to ask anyone to do it for me. I can take care of it myself. Beautiful. Nothing but the finest mineral water for my avocado-pit babies. Rich in calcium and magnesium and iron and who knows what else. They'll grow well in that.

They all walk out again, my pee emissaries. Finally I can start working on my project.

I grab the little box my mom used to transport the pits. First I need to unwrap the newspaper from around the glasses. Packed way too safely. Same way mom drives. Crawling along, coming to a full stop at every speed bump.

To avoid damage to the axles, she says. Maybe in the old days. Modern cars can take such a beating that you could drive over a speed bump at highway speed without anything happening. Says my father.

I put the eight glasses at the farthest end of the sill. Each of the eight pits I stick with three toothpicks and suspend in a glass. I start to pour in mineral water so two-thirds of each pit is submerged. But I need more liquid.

We'll see how they fare after being moved and left out of water for a day and a night. It's the first time I've taken pits on a journey. Now I need something to screen them from the view of all the people who come in and out of the room. Wasn't there a book in the drawer of the nightstand? I open the drawer. A Bible. Of course. These Christians. Always trying to get you. Not going to get me. But as a screen it'll do. I prop it up in front of the pits, open, but upside down so the cross is on its head. That'll piss them off, right? It's a sign of something bad to them. But what? Who cares.

On top of my little greenhouse I put the menu of the week's food choices. That way nobody can see my little secret from above. I'll only be getting whole-grain bread and granola anyway.

My family's all set up. The pit collection makes it feel a bit more like home. As long as I can take care of my avocados I'll have something to do. Filling them up with water or replacing the water. Documenting their progress with the camera. Once in a while scraping off the slime. Pinching off dead or blighted leaves so healthy ones can grow. That kind of thing.

The phone rings. Who had it connected? Is that something the candy stripers do? With what money? Do you have to pay for it? I'll have to look into that. I pick it up.

"Hello?"

"It's me." Mom.

Mom and dad want to visit today. They both want to avoid being there at the same time as the other.

I want so bad for my parents to be in a room together. I want them to visit me here in the hospital at the same time. I have a plan.

Mom asks, "When is your father coming?"

"You mean your ex-husband? The one you used to love so much? At four."

"Then I'll come at five. Will you make sure he's gone by then?"

I say yes but think no. As soon as I've hung up with mom, I call dad and tell him it would be good for me if he came at five.

Dad shows up at five and brings me a book about slugs.

I think maybe it's a reference to my butthole and ask about it. He says he thought I was interested in them because I asked him about them once. I'm sure I did—that's the only sort of topic I can talk about with dad.

Not about real feelings or problems. He's never figured that out. That's why I talk to him a lot about plants, animals, and environmental pollution. He would never ask how my openly gaping wound is doing. I can't think of much to talk about with him. The whole time he's sitting there in the chair at the end of my bed, I keep expecting a knock at the door followed by mom entering the room. I hate awkward pauses. Though as a personal challenge, I try to keep them going. For that, dad is the perfect partner. He doesn't talk. Unless I ask him something. He just doesn't need to talk, I guess. I look at him and he at me. It's horribly quiet. But he doesn't look unfriendly or anything. Actually quite friendly and relaxed. I have no idea why. I guess I could ask. Perhaps I'm afraid of the answer. But that's definitely not a reason to leave someone, just because he sits there, looks at you, and doesn't say anything. There must be a better reason than that. Maybe their love faded. If you really want to promise something worthwhile, try this: I will stand by you even if I no longer love you. Now that's a promise. That really means forever.

In good times and in bad. It's certainly bad times when one person no longer loves the other. To stay only as long as there is love is not good enough if you have children.

Mom comes too late. She's still not there at six. Dad leaves. Failed once again. They repel each other like two negative poles of magnets I'm trying to push together.

My goal is that they see each other and, years after separating, fall head over heels in love again. And get back together. Highly unlikely. But anything's possible. At least that's what I maintain. Though I'm not really so sure.

A lot of time elapses between dad's departure and mom's arrival. I speak even less with mom than I did with dad. She thinks I'm upset because she's late. The perpetually guilty conscience of a working mother. She doesn't know what I know. That she just missed her future husband. I don't let on. She can go ahead and try to convince herself that my bad manners have to do with my pain.

Her visit was a lot shorter than dad's. Your own fault, Helen.

They both plan to come back tomorrow. So I'll try again. The longer I stay in the hospital, the more chances I'll have to bring them together. At home I'm either at my mom's, where dad will never go, or at my dad's, where my mom will never go.

So it would be better not to have a bowel movement. For my own recovery, of course, the opposite is true—better to have a bowel movement soon, if the doctors are to be believed. I can secretly have a bowel movement and not tell anyone. That way I'll be able to stay in the hospital longer without having to worry about my bum.

That's what I'll do. Also, maybe by injuring myself again I can force another operation. Then I'd have many more days to work toward my goal.

Maybe something will occur to me. Definitely. I certainly have enough time here in my boring, atheist room to think up all sorts of possibilities. My parents were each here for only a short time. I'm not talking enough to people. I always realize I'm not when I fall into a state of brooding and start to have bad breath. When I don't talk for a long time—don't open my mouth and give it a chance to air out—the leftover bits of food and the warm saliva in my closed mouth begin to ferment. At night your mouth is the perfect, body-temperature petri dish—bacteria multiplies and the food between your teeth decays. That's what's starting to happen to me now. I need to talk to someone. I push the buzzer. Robin comes in. I have to think of a reason why I pushed the call button. Ah—a question.

"When am I getting the device from the anesthesiologist so I can self-administer pain medicine?"

"He was supposed to have been here a long time ago."

"Good. So anytime, then. Otherwise I would ask for tablets now, as the pain is starting up again."

That's a lie. But it makes my use of the call button more believable. He reaches for the door handle.

"Are you okay, Robin?"

Typical of you, Helen. He's a nurse. Yet I think I have to look after him and make sure he has a nice shift.

"Yes, I'm doing fine. I've been thinking a lot about your wound and about how cool you are about it. I even talked about it with a buddy. Don't worry—nobody from here at the hospital. He thinks you're an exhibitionist or whatever you call it."

"Show-off is what I always say. And it's true. Is that bad?"

"No, I wish more girls were that way. Like the girls I meet at clubs."

To keep the conversation going and maybe also a little to try to turn Robin on and get him into me, I tell him about my nights out.

"Do you know what I always do when I go to the disco?"

I do a cool thing when I'm meeting a boy and want to fuck him. To prove that I'm the one who initiated the fuck that night. To show that what happens later on is no coincidence. A night like that always starts out a little uncertain. You know how it is. Do you both want the same thing? Will you manage to have sex at the end of the night? Or was the date all for nothing? To make totally clear what I wanted from the get-go, I cut a big hole in my underwear so you can see the hair and the lips. Basically, the whole peach should peek out. Obviously I wear a skirt. I start to make out with him and we grab at each other. After he's stroked my breasts for long enough, at some point his finger wanders down to my thigh. He thinks he has to painstakingly work his way into my underwear and is worrying whether I want to go that far. You're not going to discuss that kind of thing when you haven't known each other long. Then, with no warning, his finger comes into direct contact with my dripping wet pussy.

Boys all react the same way to this gift. The finger has a heart attack and pauses for a second. Then there's more feeling around because he can't believe what his finger has found. They always think, She's not wearing underwear. Once they realize—like they're playing a sensory perception game—that there's a hole in the underwear, it becomes clear that I got ready for this and tinkered with them hours prior. This always causes a broad, dirty grin to spread across the face of my prospective partner. That is, my prospective fuck partner.

I break out into a bit of a sweat just telling the story. What would possess me to do this? I think I just got a rush from his compliment. Always have to dial it up a notch, eh, Helen?

Robin stands there with his mouth slightly ajar. My story has achieved its desired effect. I can see his cock bulging in his white scrubs. While I've been telling him the story, the call buzzer's been going nonstop out in the hallway. Other patients who want something from Robin. But not the same thing I want.

"Okay, see you later," he says, and leaves.

I've unsettled him. It's like a sport. In any room I have to be the most uninhibited of all those present. This time I've won. But this was an easy opponent; it wasn't even a real contest. More like a blowout.

I'm already curious what the effect will be, whether he'll still be able to look me in the eyes. I put myself in strange situations. Is it possible that *anyone* who works in a hospital—whether they're old or young, good-looking or ugly—seems sexually attractive just because there's nobody else around?

I exhale through my nose to settle my breathing. Better already. I don't have to muster the strength to get up and go brush my teeth. Just push the call button and tell filthy stories and I'll get plenty of fresh air in my mouth. In the old days children who said bad words would have their mouths washed out with soap. Did people really do that, or only threaten to do it? I'll have to try it out. I'll say a bad word and then wash my mouth out with soap. Something else to add to my mental scrapbook. I've already sprayed myself with pepper spray—also just because I wanted to know what it felt like. The brand I used was called Knockout but I know now there's no truth to the name. I didn't pass out. My eyes just started to tear up really bad and I couldn't get them to stop. You cough a lot, and spit runs out of your mouth like a waterfall. The stuff really agitates your mucous membranes. I'm bored here. I can tell from the thoughts in my head. I'm trying to entertain myself with my own old stories. I'm trying to divert attention from how lonely I feel. It's not working. Being alone scares me. Must be one of the afflictions of being a child of divorce.

I'll go to bed with any idiot just so I don't have to be in bed alone or spend a whole night sleeping alone. Anybody is better than nobody.

My parents didn't anticipate that when they split up. Adults don't think about the wide-ranging consequences of a breakup.

I sink my head deep into my pillow and look up at the ceiling. The TV hangs there. That's it. I'll play my old guess-that-voice game. I pull the remote out of the drawer and turn on the TV. Using the brightness button, I keep pushing "minus" until the picture goes dark. Then I turn up the sound and start changing channels. The idea is to pick out the voice of someone speaking. Obviously it only works with familiar people. I came up with this game because I liked to watch TV to stave off loneliness but I started to get annoyed at the shows. It had to do with one thing above all else. When people on TV have sex with each other and the woman stands up afterward, she always covers her breasts with a sheet. I just can't stand that. They've just stuck parts of themselves inside each another and now she's hiding her tits. Not from him, but from me. How am I supposed to get into what's happening on the screen when they keep reminding me that I'm watching? If the man stands up, they only show him from behind. So aggravating. That's how they lost me as a TV viewer. Only unknown actresses show their tits on TV. When somebody is running around with no top on, you can be sure she's unknown. The stars never show anything. That's the way acting is these days. Now I only listen to the TV—for my guessing game. I used to be better at it. When I was young and watched a lot of TV I recognized voices much better.

I stare at the black screen and try to concentrate on the voices. No idea whose they are. I turn off the TV again. I don't feel like playing. It's more fun to play against someone. I'll ask Robin when he has time. Which is never.

What else can you play here in this room? Something occurs to me.

I push my head back, getting the pillow under my neck, so I can look above and behind me. I haven't looked there yet. That's where the pale light is coming from. On the wall is a row of long fluorescent tubes. A wooden cover hangs in front of them to keep them from being blinding. I look at the grain of the wood and all I can see are pussies. Whenever I see the grain of boards lined up next to one another, I see pussies of all shapes and sizes. Like on the door to my room at home. It's covered with that thin wood laminate that's made in mirror-image panels. It reminds me of something from art class when I was younger. You put a blotch of watercolor and water in the middle of a piece of paper, fold it in half, press it together, then open it up again, and your pussy portrait's done. I try to conjure something else in the grain of the fluorescent light cover. Doesn't work. Just pussies. I ring the call button. What could I want now? Think of something fast.

A knock and the door opens. A female nurse walks in. Actually she opened the door first and then knocked. I'm so generous to this oafish nurse that I switch the order of the two activities in my head so she comes across as more courteous. Robin must have sent her. I've got him too flustered for now. I'll have to work on that. This nurse is named Margarete. Says so on the badge on her chest. I looked at her breasts first and then her face. I do that often. But I'm fascinated by her face. She's unbelievably well-kept. That's what people say: a well-kept woman.

As if being "well-kept" represents something of great value. At school we call kids who look like that "doctors' daughters" no matter what their fathers do. I don't know how they do it, but they always look better washed than the rest of us. Everything is clean and carefully styled. Every little body part has been treated with some beauty product.

What these women don't know: the more effort they put into these little details, the more uptight they seem. Their bearing is stiff and unsexy because they're worried about messing up all their work.

Well-kept women get their hair, nails, lips, feet, faces, skin, and hands done. Colored, lengthened, painted, peeled, plucked, shaved, and lotioned.

They sit around stiffly—like works of art—because they know how much work has gone into everything and they want it to last as long as possible.

Those type of women would never let themselves get all messy fucking.

Everything that's sexy—mussed hair, straps that fall off the shoulder, a sweaty glow on the face—is a bit askew, yes, but touchable.

Margarete looks at me questioningly. I'm supposed to tell her what the story is.

"I need a trash can for my dirty bandages. If I leave them on the nightstand it won't smell too good in here."

Very convincing, Helen. Well done.

She's sympathetic to my put-on wish for additional hygiene in the hospital room, says "of course," and walks out.

I hear noise outside. Something's happening. Probably nothing exciting. The usual hospital things. I bet it has to do with distributing dinner. Here in the hospital you're subject to a strict schedule that must have been designed by a lunatic. Starting at six in the morning the nurses bounce loudly around the hallways. They come in with coffee, they want to clean the room or clean me. You're trapped in a beehive full of worker bees, all flying around and tending to something. Very loudly most of the time. All sick people really want to do is sleep, and that's the one thing they won't let you do here. If after a bad night—and every night is bad in a hospital—I want to catch up on sleep, there are at least eight people conspiring against my doing this. Nobody who works in the hospital pays attention to whether someone is sleeping when they enter the room. They all just yell "Morning" and loudly do whatever it is they have to do. They could just drop the "Morning" and quietly and considerately take care of their duties in the room. They have something against sleep here. I heard once that you're not supposed to let people with depression sleep too much because it intensifies the depression. But this isn't a nuthouse. I sometimes think they use the constant interruptions to make sure the patients are still alive. As soon as one nods off, he has to be saved from certain death: "Morning!"

People come in and out. Each one expects me to be understanding. But that should go both ways. That's how the world works.

The nurse comes back in with a little chrome trash can and sets it on the nightstand. She pushes down on the plastic pedal with her hand and the top flies open. I put in the used bandages from between my ass cheeks. The way Margarete uses the pedal is typical of a well-kept woman. She pays close attention to her nails. She touches everything only with her fingertips. Odd phenomenon. Sure, if your nails have just been painted, you're careful not to touch things until they dry. But some women act the same way even when their nails are dry. It makes them look squeamish. As if they're disgusted by everything around them.

"Thanks a lot. When it comes to hygiene, I'm quite particular," I say with a broad smile.

She nods knowingly—though she doesn't know a thing. She thinks I want to keep things neat here, that the smell bothers me, or that I'm ashamed of the bandages I magically pull out of my behind. In reality, what I'm quite particular about when it comes to hygiene is that I don't give a shit about it, and I despise germaphobes like Margarete.

What's up with me? Why am I so worked up about her? She's hasn't done anything to me.

I'm putting one over on her with my trash can request, not the other way around. When I instantly despise someone for no comprehensible reason, when I want to punch them or at the very least insult them in the harshest terms, it usually means my period is on the way. Just to top it all off.

Margarete says, "Have fun with your trash can."

Yeah. Thanks a lot. You're a barrel of laughs.

I've already lost plenty of blood down there. And I've already got plenty to do to take care of my wounded ass without having to worry about preventing the flow of blood from my period, too. I'm fine with my actual period once the irritability right before it dissipates. Often I'm horny when I'm bleeding.

One of the first dirty sayings I ever heard, when I was very young, was at a party my parents threw, and I had to ask around a lot before I understood it: It's okay to swim in the red river as long as you don't drink the water.

It used to be considered disgusting for a man to fuck a woman who was bleeding. But those days are long gone. When I fuck a boy who likes it when I'm bleeding, we leave behind a huge, blood-splattered mess in the bed.

When I have any control over the particulars, I try to get fresh, white sheets to use. And I change positions and move around the bed as much as possible so there's blood all over the place.

When we're fucking I like to be sitting or squatting so gravity helps as much blood as possible flow out of my pussy. If I simply lie there, the blood just pools.

I also love it when someone goes down on me while I'm bleeding. It's kind of a test of mettle for the guy. When he's finished licking and looks up with his blood-smeared mouth, I kiss him so we both look like wolves who've just ripped open a deer.

I like to have the taste of blood in my mouth when we finally fuck. I find it extremely exciting, and I'm always sad when after a few wolf-days my period ends.

But I'm lucky. From what I hear from other girls, some of them are in pain for days on end. Doesn't exactly make you want to have sex.

All that happens to me is that shortly before it starts, I get into a really bad mood—like right now—and I'm extremely aggressive toward random people I encounter. Then the blood starts to flow. No pain. No cramps.

Back when periods were still something new to me, I used to think I really was just in a bad mood. And then I'd be caught by surprise by the blood. Usually in school. Clearly visible to everyone as a red stain on the back of my skirt, because I'd be sitting when it started. You're always sitting in school.

Or during a visit with my relatives at my aunt's house. I went to bed because I didn't feel well. I didn't know why.

The next morning I got up and saw that I'd covered the bed with blood. A huge puddle. I was too self-conscious to go to my aunt and say that I'd had a bit of an accident. There was just nothing I could do.

I had slept and hadn't noticed anything. I didn't know how to describe what had happened to me, either. I decided just not to say anything. I left the next morning like nothing had happened, leaving the mess behind without comment.

My aunt must have gone into the room to tidy up and noticed it right away. I hadn't even covered it with the blanket. All those liters of red were right out in the open for my aunt to see. Ever since then I've been uptight around my aunt. Though she's never said anything about it.

Typical of family.

I can't think of anything else when I see her. Until I get so ashamed I can hear the blood pulsing in my ears.

When it comes to my period, I don't care about hygiene, either. It's blown completely out of proportion. Tampons are expensive and unnecessary. When I have my period, I use toilet paper to make my own tampons while I'm sitting on the toilet. I'm proud of that.

I've developed a special balling and packing technique so they stay in for a long time and hold in the blood. But I have to admit that my toilet paper tampons really just stop up my pussy and dam up the blood rather than absorbing it the way commercial tampons do. I asked my gynecologist, though, whether it was harmful to the pussy to keep the blood inside and then let it flow out while sitting on the toilet. And he said it was a common misconception that the bleeding had some kind of purifying effect. So from a medical perspective, my blood-dam system is harmless.

A few times I went to the gynecologist because I'd lost a tampon inside me. I was sure I'd stuffed one in but, when I went to pull it out, I couldn't find it anymore. Of course, that's a small disadvantage of my homemade tampons: there's no turquoise-colored string to pull it out with. And my fingers are kind of short, so I don't get too far when I'm looking for something in my pussy.

A couple of times when I found myself in this situation at my dad's house, I had to fish around in there with his nice barbecue tongs. There's usually charred bits of meat and fat stuck to them. I couldn't be bothered to clean the tongs before they went inside me. So I laid myself down in Dr. Broekert position and tried as best I could to locate the clump of toilet paper in my pussy. With all the stuff from the grill still on them. Often without finding anything. Just as I don't clean the tongs before I shove them inside me, I don't wash them before they land back on dad's grill after my gynecological insertion. I always have a broad grin on my face during barbecues with friends of the family.

I ask everyone "Doesn't it taste great?" and wave to my father who waves back with the tongs, smiling. My third hobby. Spreading bacteria.

If I'm unsuccessful in my search with the barbecue tongs and start to worry that the bloody toilet paper will rot inside me and I'll die a horrible death from infection, I go to the gynecologist.

He calls it my Bermuda Triangle problem. Sometimes he can help me, but often he can't find anything, either. He has really long fingers and all kinds of medical barbecue tongs made out of steel. And still there are times when he doesn't find the clumps.

"Are you sure you inserted a tampon?"

Cute. He always says "inserted." I always say "shoved in."

"Yes, absolutely sure."

I'm a real mystery to him. As my pussy is to me. I have no idea where the clumps go. Hopefully I'll live long enough to figure out this mystery. Dr. Broekert does an ultrasound to make sure there's nothing hiding up there.

Often I'm too lazy to craft new tampons. So I don't throw away the old one—that took me so long to fold up— in the toilet every time I go to the bathroom. I pull it out with my finger after I've sat down. And I put it on the floor. The dirtier the floor, the better.

If I can add a bloodstain to all the other stains on the floor, great. Once I'm finished with whatever I had to do on the toilet, I grab it off the floor and shove it back in. I like the smell of old blood that's gushed out of my pussy.

But then, I like the smell of truffles. I've heard horror stories about what happens if you don't always replace your tampon regularly. You get the worst infection—some women even die from toxic shock. Since I've been getting my period—that is, for six years —this is how I've dealt with my body and my pussy and my bacteria, and my gynecologist hasn't had any moments of anguish over me.

I used to have a close friend, Irene. I always called her Sirene. It suited her better. And we came up with a cool idea: Whenever we had our period at the same time—which didn't happen very often, as you can imagine—we would do the following.

Each of us in a stall. Just a divider between us. The usual eight-inch gap between the base of the divider and the floor. We both take out our tampons—back then they were minis with light-turquoise strings—and then, one, two, three, go, we'd pass each other our tampons beneath the divider. And then, when we were finished peeing and dabbing ourselves dry, we each shoved in the other's tampon. Through our old, stinky blood, we were bound together like Old Shatterhand and Winnetou. Blood sisters.

Sirene's tampon always looked interesting. Before I stuck it in each time, I would examine it closely. Very different from mine. Who knows what another girl's used tampon looks like? Okay, okay. Who even wants to know? Besides me. I know.

Recently during one of my exciting trips to a brothel, I learned something else about bleeding and tampons. I go to brothels a lot now to explore the female body. It's not like I can ask my mother or my friends. Whether they'll spread open their pussies for me so I can satisfy my thirst for knowledge. Couldn't bring myself to do that.

Now that I'm eighteen, I can show my ID and get into a brothel. I look way younger, so they always ask to see it. My life has gotten a lot better since I turned eighteen, but also a lot more expensive. First the sterilization. That was nine-hundred euros including the anesthesia. Here in this same hospital. I paid for it myself. Now all the visits to the brothel. I have to earn it all working for the racist at the market.

Older men always take guys to brothels on their eighteenth birthdays so they can have their first hooker-fuck. In the old days it was probably their first fuck of any kind. These days there's no way that's the case.

I waited patiently until my eighteenth birthday, but nobody offered to take me there. So I did it all by myself. I found the numbers of brothels in our town, called them up, and, with hope in my voice, asked them whether any of the hookers working there dealt with women. Not many did.

One of the brothels, though, immediately said it had a large selection of hookers open to women. It's called the Sauna Oasis. The madam said it would be better if I came early in the evening as the male johns often got annoyed at female johns. Or do you call them johnettes? Whatever.

I was okay with that and now I go there often.

I wanted to pick out the right hooker for me in the waiting room. She looked like a black version of me. By that I mean she was built like me. Thin, small breasts, a wide, flat ass, but overall petite. And long, straight hair. But I think her hair was made out of plastic. Island braid extensions. I went over to her. I already knew she was willing to go with women. That didn't need to be discussed. When I'm picking, the only women in the waiting room are ones there for me, a female client. All those who service only men—maybe on religious grounds?—disappear into a backroom while I'm selecting. I go over to her, as determined as possible. I feel very awkward in this brothel setting. No wonder men always have to get hopelessly drunk before they get up the nerve to go. And then they can't get it up or can't remember their expensive fuck afterward. You really feel as if you're doing something unbelievably taboo, something crazy. I wish I were drunk, too, when I'm there. But I worry I won't remember afterward what the pussies look like. In which case it would all have been for nothing. That's why I'm doing this, after all. Studying pussy. So I go sober. I have too much respect for the women there and for the situation. I look forward to a time when I don't feel so uncomfortable anymore, once I've gotten used to it. At the moment I still get a lump in my throat and my heart races. Only after a few minutes with one of the women do I start to chill out. Back to that first time with the girl who looks like me. I ask her what her name is.

"Milena."

I tell her my name.

She asks me in front of all the other hookers whether I have my period. What made her think that? I think I know. She smelled it through my pants. I had a school friend from Poland whose nose was so sensitive she could tell from her seat who in the class was having their period. She fascinated me. She was like a dog. I got a real kick out of her skill. Almost every day I would ask her who was bleeding. She didn't like knowing and was disgusted by bleeding girls. She didn't want to be near them. Unfortunately, she moved back to Poland. Girls who for stupid reasons of preserving their virginity used pads were easier for her to smell. Because they carried their blood around all day on a platter. With girls who trapped their blood inside with devirginizing tampons, she had to work a little harder. But she'd sniff them out. And now they've sniffed me out here.

I answer her with a yes. She says she doesn't want to fuck me because of AIDS. Great. A few of the hookers giggle.

Milena smiles and says she has an idea. "Come with me. Have you ever heard of sponges?"

"The things you wash up with?"

She nods yes. Things are looking up, I think.

What does she have in mind? I follow her into a room. Number four. Is this her room? Or do they share rooms? I'll ask everything in the half hour I have ahead of me. For fifty euros. I can't decide what would be more enjoyable: to fuck a hooker or to ask her about all the things men have done with her or that she has done with them. Actually, each possibility turns me on as much as the other. But both at the same time—fucking and quizzing her—would be the best of all.

Naked, as she already is, she walks in her high-heeled shoes over to a cabinet and pulls out a big cardboard box. I have a chance to take a long look at her from behind. I love her ass. When she goes down on me, I'm going to bore my finger deep into her ass the whole time. What she's holding in her hands is a family-pack of something. She takes one out—it's something I've never seen before. A round piece of foam packed in clear plastic. Looks like a fortune cookie, only soft.

"This is a sponge. When we have our periods we're not allowed to work because of the risk of infection. And if we use normal tampons, the clients can feel them with their cocks. Tampons are too hard. We shove these sponges as far inside our pussies as we can and it holds the blood out of the way for a while. The sponges are so soft no cock in the world is going to notice it touching its tip. It feels just like your cunt—even to a finger. You can try it. Lie down. I'll push it in. Then I'll go down on you, even though you have your period."

Milena swims in the red river and drinks the water. And she says "cunt," too. I wouldn't dare.

I've asked in all the drugstores and pharmacies. You can't get sponges as a normal person. Maybe you need some kind of proof of prostitution or something. I could definitely use sponges. Because not every guy I fuck likes to dip into the red river. In those cases I could hide the blood the good old hooker way. Otherwise I miss out on a fuck here or there when I have to confess to blood-averse boys I've got my period. Sometimes Helen is out of luck.

By the way, another thing that really needs to stop is the way my period always sneaks up on me by surprise.

I am constantly surprised by it. It was true before I was on the pill, and it's still true now that I'm on the pill—obviously no longer to prevent pregnancy but to prevent pimples. My period never comes regularly or when it's supposed to. Never the way it's described on the package. It's made a mess of every single pair of my underwear. Particularly the white ones. When I bleed in them and have to walk around for a while, the blood has a chance to really soak in at body temperature and then it won't come out even if you wash them on the hottest setting. Even if you were to wash the white underwear in boiling water. No chance.

So my entire collection of underwear has a brown stain right in the middle. You get used to it after a few years. Do other people have it, too? What girl or woman could I ask? None. It's always the same. With everything I really want to know.

There are probably other, more hygiene-obsessed, girls who run around their entire lives wearing panty liners to protect their underwear from their own discharges.

But I'm not one of them. I'd rather have everything stained with blood than do that.

Those girls definitely don't have the nice light-yellow crust in their crotch, either, which during the course of the day gets thicker as it continually gets re-moistened.

Sometimes a bit of the crust will hang like a dreadlock from your pubic hair, spun around the hair like pollen on a bee's leg by the rubbing motions of walking.

I like to pull this pollen off and eat it. It's a delicacy.

I just can't keep my fingers off anything on my body. I find a use for everything. If I notice a booger has slowly hardened in my nose, I have to pick it out.

When I was little I would do this in class. Even today I don't see anything wrong about someone eating boogers. There's no way it's unhealthy. I see people all the time on the highway who, when they think they aren't being watched, pop a snack from their nose into their mouth.

In school you get teased for it and quickly stop doing it. At some point I quit doing it except at home, either alone or in front of my boyfriend. I thought it was only reasonable. It's a part of me after all, this habit. But I could see in his eyes that he couldn't deal with it.

Since then I've maintained a second life in the bathroom. Whenever I piss or take a crap, I munch my nose empty of boogers. Creates a liberating sensation in your nose. But that's not the main reason I do it. If I can grab a dry booger and, by picking it out, manage to set something in motion and pull out a long piece of snot attached to it, it turns me on. Similar to pulling out the hairs stuck in my pussy. Or the crust on a pubic hair. It hurts and it turns me on. And all of it makes its way into my mouth and gets slowly chewed with my front teeth so I can really taste it. I don't need any tissues. I'm my own garbage disposal. Bodily secretion recycler. I get the same thrill out of cleaning my ears with cotton swabs. Sticking them in a little too deep.

That's another distinct childhood memory. I'm sitting on the rim of the bathtub and my mother is cleaning my ears with a cotton swab dipped in warm water. A nice, tingling feeling that immediately turns to pain if you go in too far. I'm constantly told that I shouldn't use cotton swabs because you might pack the earwax in and damage the ear. And that it's bad to use cotton swabs too often because your

ears will be too clean and the earwax is necessary to protect the inner ear. I don't care. I don't do it to clean my ears
but to get myself off. More than once a day. Preferably on
the toilet.

Back to the hygiene freaks. They throw out the lovely
crust with their panty liners each time they go to the bathroom and have to start collecting it all over again from
scratch.

And I'm sure these girls never forget they're about to
get their period. Even while in pain in the hospital. The
highest imperative in their lives: leave no stains. With me
it's the opposite.

It's starting to flow, the blood. I knew it. I take the giant
Tupperware container off the windowsill, put it on my lap,
and root around in it until I've found some gauze squares. I
estimate them to be about four inches by four inches. I decide to experiment and instead of making a tampon out of
toilet paper as usual, I make one out of gauze.

It should be easier, and unlike toilet paper it should
be absorbant. We'll see. I pull out a square and put the container back on the windowsill. I fold one side a little bit so
I have a starting point to roll it up. Now it looks like a sausage. Then I fold it over like a horseshoe or a long apple
strudel, so it fits in the oven with the thick, folded side
shoved as deep in my pussy as possible.

Whenever I can cheat the tampon industry, it makes me feel good.

I smell the finger I used to stuff in my homemade tampon. I can already detect a musty pussy scent.

At one of my numerous brothel visits a hooker told me that some men get off on coming in with their cocks dirty and making a hooker suck them off. She said it was a power game. Those are their least favorite clients, the dirty ones. The purposefully dirty ones. They don't have anything against inadvertently dirty ones.

I wanted to try that, too. I didn't wash myself for a long time and then had a hooker go down on me. For me there was nothing different about it from having someone go down on me when I'm clean. Power games aren't my thing.

What can I do now to divert my attention from my numbing loneliness?

I guess I could try to think of all the useful things I've learned over the course of my young life. I can entertain myself well that way—at least for a few minutes.

I once had a really old lover. I love to say "lover." It sounds so old-fashioned. Better than "fucker." He was many, many years older than me. I learned a lot from him. He wanted me to experience everything about male sexuality so that in the future no man could ever pull one over on me. Now I supposedly know a lot about male sexuality, but I don't know whether all of what I learned applies to all men or only to him. I still have to see. One of his cardinal rules was that you should always stick your finger up a guy's ass during sex. Makes him come harder. So far I can certainly concur. It's always a hit. They go wild. But you shouldn't discuss it with them beforehand or after. Otherwise they'll worry they're gay and get all uptight. Just do it and afterward pretend nothing was ever in there.

This older boyfriend also showed me lots of porn films. He thought not only could men learn a lot from them, but women, too. It's true.

It was in one of those films that I saw a black woman's pussy for the first time. That's something. Because they have dark skin, the interior colors of the pussy really pop when it's spread open. Much more than with white women, where the contrast isn't as extreme. Something to do with complementary colors, I think. Pussy-pink next to light-pink skin tone looks a lot more boring than pussy-pink next to dark-brown skin tone. Against dark brown the pussy-pink looks dark-lavender-bluish-red. Swollen and throbbing.

I'm telling you. Complementary colors. Brown skin complements pussy-pink.

It impressed me so much that since then I always put makeup on the inside of my pussy when I have a date to fuck. I use standard makeup that you'd normally put on your face. I have yet to find pussy makeup at the drugstore. A gap in the market.

Like when you're putting makeup on your eyes, I make it darker the closer you get to the center. I start with light pink and pink tones, lip gloss and eye shadow, and work my way through the folds until I'm right at the entrance to the tunnel, where I use dark red, lavender, and blue. I like to color the brown-pink of the rosette with a few dabs of lipstick, too, rubbing it on with my finger.

It makes the pussy and rosette more dramatic, deeper, more beguiling.

Since I learned that black women have the reddest pussies, I only go to black hookers. There are no other black women in my world—not in my school, not in my neighborhood. Prostitution is my only chance. I'm sure plenty of men understand my problem.

I had a really bad experience with a white hooker. She had skin as pale as cheese and light-red hair. She was a little chubby and—totally unnecessarily—completely shaved. And I mean everything was bare. Not a single pubic hair anywhere. Her crotch looked like a sculpture of a newborn baby made out of cheese.

I had been looking forward to her tits. From beneath her shirt they made a good impression. Big but still pointing upward. When she undressed and took off her bra, it was a big disappointment. She had big droopy breasts with flat nipples.

Flat nipples are something really bad.

All a nipple is supposed to do is stick out. Flat nipples don't do that. It's as if someone had pushed the nipple back into the breast and it stayed there, cowering in fear. Like a little collapsed soufflé.

I thought, well I'm already here and I'm going to have to pay so I might as well close my eyes and go for it. Some of the hookers had told me that men who weren't happy with their hooker once she got naked just walked back out without paying and picked a different one. I could never do that. I'm too much of a beginner—and too polite.

I would have to tell her to her face that she didn't look good. I'd rather not. I wouldn't have the heart.

I convince myself that it's also an important experience to have sex with someone I find ugly, and immediately
I go down on her on the bed.

She puts her hands behind her head and does nothing. I'm doing all the work. I lick her and grind my pussy on
her bent knee. I come fast. I'm the queen of grinding. She
hasn't moved an inch the entire time. A very lazy hooker.
Didn't know there was such a thing.

After I've come, she starts looking around for something to munch on. Finds something. She knocks back a
glass of the expensive champagne I paid for and munches
on goldfish crackers. She can't believe how fast I came and
asks whether I've ever had anal sex.

I don't understand why she's asking. But I answer truth-
fully and say yes.

"How is it? Doesn't it hurt?"

What? Who's the hooker here? I decide that as a young
client it's not my job to explain anal sex to a hooker. I leave.
But I pay. I did come, after all, even if the collapsed soufflés
were no help at all. It was simple mechanics.

The hookers are always older than me—even the young-
est ones. That's why I always assume they've had more experience than me when it comes to sexual experimentation. But
that's not the case. They limit what they do professionally.
They'll say, for instance, no kissing and no anal. So they never
learn anything new. I suppose they have their reasons.

Maybe there are a lot of johns who don't properly pre-pare the asshole before they fuck it. That can hurt. And guys like that probably pretend not to notice the pain they're causing, and that makes it hurt even worse.

Depending on how long and thick the cock is that's supposed to go up there, I like to take plenty of time to stretch it out, or at least have a lot of alcohol or something else numbing.

Anal sex is great—even though sometimes you don't notice until the next day that you overestimated your abil-ity to stretch.

Overall it was a bad experience with the redhead. Now whenever I see a light-skinned redhead, I chuckle inside and think to myself she's lazy in bed, has no hair—anywhere, like an alien—eats goldfish and has never had anything up her ass. And her nipples don't stick out.

My dad, drunk at a party, once said to a redhead friend of my mother's, "Ginger hair, always moist down there."

Not at all!

And now, Helen? What are you going to do now? Got a plan?

I could look out the window and ponder nature for a while. It's summer. The chestnut trees in the hospital yard are in full bloom. Someone—probably a landscaper—has made planters by cutting off the top halves of what look like big, green-plastic trash barrels. If I'm seeing them correctly from this distance, they're planted with fuschia and bleeding-heart flowers. Those are my favorites. It sounds so romantic. Bleeding-heart. My father taught me the name. I remember everything my father has taught me. Always. The things my mother's taught me, not so much. But my father doesn't try to teach me things as often—maybe that makes the lessons easier to remember. My mother blathers on all day about things I'm supposed to remember. Things she thinks are important for me. Half of it I forget immediately; as for the other half, I purposefully do the opposite. My father teaches me things that are important to him. Everything about plants. He'll say out of the blue: "Did you know you should dig up dahlias in the fall and let them winter over in the basement? And that you plant them again early in the year in the garden?"

Of course I didn't know that. But duly noted, now I do. Dad derives great pleasure from knowing so much about the natural world. Mom's afraid of the natural world and her knowledge of it. She always seems to be fighting against it. She fights against dirt in the household. She fights against various insects. In the garden, too. Fights against bacteria of all kinds. Against sex. Against men and against women. There seems to be nothing my mother isn't bothered by. She once told me that sex with my father caused her pain. That his penis was too big for her insides. This is not information I wanted to know. Wait, I was actually hoping to focus on the natural world outside the hospital. That'll put me in a better mood than pondering sexual intercourse between my parents. Unfortunately, I always picture things in intricate detail. Sometimes the images aren't very pretty.

Helen, kill these thoughts of yours.

Boredom is creeping back.

Mom always says, "Boring people are bored."

Oh well. She also says, "We aren't put on this earth to be happy."

Not your kids, anyway, mom.

Try again, Helen. If you're bored, you can always make a date with yourself to look out the window. Good idea. Busy yourself getting to know your environment. No reason to stay fixated on things down below. Now would be a good time.

I snap my head to the side and stare out the window.

Lawn. Trees. Chestnuts. What else? I see a huge staghorn sumac tree. I guess I don't even have to say it's big. Staghorn sumac trees are always big. They scare me. My father taught me that, too. To be scared of staghorn sumac trees. They're not from here. They're not native. Asian or something. And they grow a lot faster than our trees. When they're still small—which is the case for only a short period—they send up a long, thin, rubberlike trunk that puts all its energy into gaining height.

That way they overtake all the surrounding plants. Once they've exceeded the height of everything around them, they sprout a broad crown over everything else. That kills everything else had been growing beneath it—light no longer gets through, and the roots of the fast-growing staghorn sumac suck up all the water.

But it's not all bad. Since the trunk shoots up so fast, it's unstable compared to our trees. Entire branches break off in the slightest breeze. Serves it right. But the branches often hit people who don't realize they're standing under an Asian tree unable to withstand wind because it busies itself trying to outpace everything else in terms of height and forgets to build a sturdy base for itself.

I always walk in a wide arc around staghorn sumac trees. I wouldn't want one of them to become the epitaph on my gravestone.

When I walk the streets, I see staghorn sumacs all over the place. They seem to grow out of every crack in the earth. They propagate like mad. The city government must be constantly removing them—otherwise they would have completely taken over long ago. Sometimes I notice people who have let one grow in their garden after it appeared. They have no one to blame but themselves. Soon it'll be the only thing in the garden. But I can't ring all of their doorbells and warn them. That would be too much work. Unfortunately, not everyone has a father like mine who can teach them such useful things.

The staghorn sumac fronds are big. In the middle a long stem, at the top end a little leaflet like a head, and then a series of very symmetrical lance-shaped leaflets along each side. Left and right, like ribs. I'll pick out a branch from here and count the leaflets. I've got to do something. Twenty-five leaflets on one frond. Eagle-eyed Helen. Not really— like I said, they're big. Too big. The trunk is smooth and greenish. It looks like uncut brown bread. It feels nice—if you're brave enough to walk under one and touch it.

Enough about nature. My turn again. For a while now I've felt something on my right upper arm. I'm going to look at it. I shift my shoulder forward, grab the fat on my upper arm, and roll it toward me. Now I can see it. Just as I thought —a blackhead. I have no idea why my upper arm is full of them. My own poor explanation for it goes like this: hair tries to grow there but because of the friction from T-shirt sleeve edges, individual hairs stay under the skin and get infected.

And so I come to one of my biggest hobbies. Popping zits. I've noticed a big blackhead in Robin's ear. More precisely in the flat area just outside the ear hole. I've often seen people with exceptionally large, black things like that right in the same area. I think people just don't tell each other and the blackhead then has years to fill itself with dirt and grease. Several times I've forgotten to ask people ahead of time and have just reached for their zit in order to pop it. I practically grabbed Robin's ear. I could barely control myself. But a lot of people aren't cool with that. When you just pop their zit without asking. They think it's overstepping a boundary. I'll ask Robin, though, once we know each other better. I'm sure we'll get to know each other better. Not going to escape. The blackhead in Robin's ear, I mean. That's reserved for me. I clench the blackhead on my upper arm between the thumb and pointer finger of my left hand and, with a squeeze, out comes the worm.

It goes directly from my thumb into my mouth.

With that taken care of, I examine the little wound.

There's a drop of blood in the hole left behind by the blackhead.

I wipe it off. It doesn't disappear. It just smears.

Just like on my legs when I've shaved them instead of Kanell. Fast and careless. Often I get goose bumps from the cold water and from standing around in the tub. When I shave over them, I tear open every bump. Then I think I looked better with hair because now there's a pinpoint of blood where every hair was. At some point I put on a pair of nylons over my bleeding legs and discovered an interesting effect. The almost see-through, skin-color nylons smeared each speck of blood into a stripe as I pulled them up my legs. By the time I had them all the way up, they looked like an expensive pair of patterned nylons. I wear them that way a lot when I go out.

Wearing nylons over my bloody legs has another advantage, too. I like to eat my scabs. At the end of a night out, when I take the nylons off again, they rip off the dried blood, and new scabs form. Then, once they've hardened, I can pick them off and eat them.

Tastes almost as good as sleepy seeds. The snack brought by the sandman and left in the corner of your eye closest to your nose.

When I treat my little wounds so poorly, eventually a pore or two will get sealed and keep a hair from coming out. The hair still grows, but it coils up beneath the skin. Like the roots of the avocado in the base of the glass. At some point it gets infected and then Helen enters the game. I've been very patient. Despite the fact that the whole time the hair was calling to me, "Get me out of here, I want to grow straight like the other hairs, in the fresh air," I've kept my fingers off it. It's difficult. But it's worth the wait.

First I stick a needle into the infected lump and squeeze out the pus. From my fingertip into my mouth with that. Then it's the hair's turn. I poke around in the wound as long as it takes to get at the hair. It always looks a bit stunted since it's never seen the light of day and has had to grow in tight quarters. I grab it with tweezers and pull it slowly out with the infected root. Done. Often another little pleasure will grow in the same spot a few weeks later.

A magpie is hopping across the shortly cropped hospital lawn. In children's books magpies steal shiny objects like bottle stoppers, aluminum foil, and rings. In reality they steal eggs from small songbirds. They peck them open and slurp them out. I always try to picture just how a magpie hacks a hole in the shell of a songbird's egg and then uses its beak as a straw to suck out the egg. Or do they do it completely differently? Jump on the egg until it breaks and slurp the puddle of goop off the ground?

Eggs are a constant theme with me. Years ago kids would chant, "Go climb a pole, you egg hole." For no reason; just because it rhymes. But I always read a lot into it.

I told Kanell once what I thought it meant, and one afternoon we acted it out.

The pussy was the hole, obviously.

Into it an egg. For egg hole.

At first we tried a raw egg. But it broke in Kanell's hand at the entrance to the pussy. The pieces of shell didn't cut me or anything. It's just that everything was covered in goop, and it was cold.

So then we discussed whether it had to be a raw egg. Actually it didn't. So we boiled one. Hard. Eight minutes. Very hard.

And inserted it. So I finally had the egg hole I'd always imagined from this playground rhyme.

Since then it's been our inside secret. In the most literal sense of the phrase.

There's one other thing I'd like to do with Kanell.

I've always loved to play around with the lymph nodes in my groin. I slide them around under my skin. The same way you can move your kneecap around. Recently I've had the desire for Kanell to trace them with a Sharpie. To accentuate them. The same way you accentuate your eyes with makeup. Is that a sexual fantasy? Or just a new form of body art? It would only be a fantasy if thinking of it made me hot. And that it does. What would happen the first time the fantasy were realized? He's good about exploring my fantasies, just as I've supported his with every fiber of my being, right from the start.

Out on the lawn one magpie is fighting with another. Over what?

We humans think of magpies as evil animals because they eat the young of other birds. But we eat the babies of almost every animal that appears on our menus. Lamb, veal, suckling pig.

Outside, Robin is strolling with a female nurse. The magpies fly off. I look at the two of them, appalled. I'm jealous. No way. I feel a claim to him just because he's taken a picture of my wounded ass and I gave him a titillating lecture about modifying my underwear. And because the nurse can walk and I can't. Well, I can, but only very, very slowly. They're both smoking. And laughing. What is there to laugh about?

I want to be able to walk again. I'm going to walk right now—to the cafeteria. There is one here, right Helen? Yes. The candy striper said something about it. I'm going to slowly go to the cafeteria and get a cup of coffee. Good, Helen, do something normal. Don't think anymore about Robin and his fuck-pie or about my parents in bed boning each other. I have plenty of time. Good idea. I should have been capable of thinking of it without the two strolling strangers. Coffee always makes me have to go to the bathroom. I'd like to secretly have a bowel movement, without telling anyone here. Just for me. Just so I know I still can and that I haven't grown together and sealed shut. I won't tell anyone. That way I can still use this venue to try to bring my parents together. That way the things that are supposed to be together will grow together.

I roll onto my stomach and let my legs slowly drop to the floor. I grab a painkiller from my pill supply and slurp it down. I'll get some use out of it along the way. Inside, I'm prepared for the long voyage. But not on the outside. I'm still wearing just this tree-top angel outfit, still gathered and knotted at the front. Nothing on the bottom. You can't walk around like this, even in a hospital, Helen. Even as an ass patient. There are a lot of people running around the halls and in the cafeteria. I go at a snail's pace to the space-saving, built-in wardrobe. Mom said she had left things for me in there. I open the door. Only pajama bottoms and T-shirts. I'll never be able to manage that. To put on a pair of pajama bottoms you have to bend down and put in first one leg and then the other. Oh, man. That'll stretch my ass too much. Mom didn't think of a bathrobe or something simple like that. Now what, Helen? I walk slowly back to the bed and pull off the sheet. I wrap it around myself and tie it at the shoulder so I look like a Roman on the way to the public baths. This is fine for walking around a hospital. The two ass-piss stains could have been caused by something else. They could be the result of my drooling on the sheet while sucking on a Werther's Original. Very believable, Helen. Nobody's going to ask you about it. People aren't like that. They don't want to know.

Off we go. To the door. I haven't left this room in three days. Am I even allowed to wander around? Come on, I'm not going to get in trouble for walking. But am I allowed to walk in the hall as slowly as a dying grandmother? If someone catches me, they can send me right back. Better not to ask in advance. Open the door. There's a lot going on in the hallway. Everyone is busy doing something. They all seem to know each other here, and everyone is laughing and pushing things around. To my eyes it looks as if they're doing things just to look as if they're busy in case the supervisor happens to walk past. They don't want to be caught smoking in the nurses' station. Better to chat on the hallway while shifting something around. They can't fool me. I creep past them. Nobody acknowledges me. I think I'm going so slow they can't see me with their hurried glances.

It's just as bright in the hallway as in my room. The linoleum reflects the light back up from the floor. It looks like gray water. I walk on the water. It must have something to do with the pain medication. I still know the way to the elevator. You retain that even over the course of several days. The escape route. I lie there in bed the whole time in pain and know exactly how to get out—without even being conscious of the fact that I know. Out and around to the left. There are bad religious paintings hung all over the place. The nurses probably put them up to please their parents. They all end up here sooner or later. The parents. Proctology unit. Oncology. Palliative care. Something will bring them here. Unless they care for them at home, which I think is the best way.

I bend over and hold my stomach because I can't reach my ass in this position. It hurts. I've made it to the glass door of the central part of the building. I just have to pound the buzzer like Robin and the giant glass door will open automatically. I stand there and don't go through. I have no money with me. Crap. Have to go back the whole way. No one acknowledges me on the way back, either. I guess I am allowed to wander around. I'm also allowed to take care of my wound myself. It's in an extremely unhygienic spot. Pretty much the most unhygienic spot Robin can imagine. Room 218. Mine. Open the door and in I go. Back to peace and quiet. Thanks to my idiotic forgetfulness I've wasted a

lot of energy. I look in the drawer of my metal nightstand.
There are a few small bills in it. Mom must have put them
in there while I was sleeping. Or did she tell me she had?
Or did I dream it? My memory's gone to shit. In any event,
I've got money now. I hold it in my hand as I walk. They
don't make sheets with pockets yet. My ass is getting used
to the motion. I'm a bit quicker now than on the first trip.
Probably because the pills are taking effect. I stare at the
floor the whole way. We'll see how far I get before someone comments on my attire. I punch the button. The automatic door swings open and this time I go through. Beyond
is a whole new world. Here different diseases mingle. Ass
patients and ass nurses aren't the only ones out and about.
An old woman with tubes in her nose is walking around.
The tubes run into a backpack that's attached to a walker.

   She obviously has something wrong with her head—
not a proctology case. That's a change of pace. She has beautiful white hair that's in a long braid coiled on top of her head.
And a nice bathrobe on. Black with three-dimensional pink
flowers on it. And nice slippers. Made of black velvet. You
can see the shape of a bunion through the slippers. Like a
tumor on her big toe. It's growing sideways over the other
toes. And by doing that it pushes the joint of the big toe
farther and farther to the outside. Until it's quite far away
from the rest of the foot. A bunion like that is a destructive
force. It bursts out of all your shoes over time. It's about to

destroy those velvet slippers. The toes end up like teeth in a jaw, crowding and displacing each other and becoming crooked. But the big toe always wins the battle. I know it. I have a bunion, too. Everyone in our family does. Father's and mother's side. Very bad genes, all things considered. The big toe always wants to go where the other toes belong, so little toes keep having to be surgically removed. My uncle, my grandmother, and my mother hardly have any toes left. Their feet end up looking like devil's hooves.

I want to think about something nicer so I try to find a pleasant end to my granny observations.

Okay, even her spider veins are pretty. I used to call these weblike formations varicose veins. But they're actually called spider veins. Everything about her is pretty. Except for the bunion and the tubes. The tubes will soon be taken out, I'm sure. Hopefully she won't have to die with them in.

I push the button for the elevator, cross my fingers for the handsome old woman, and say hello to her very loudly. In case she's already hard of hearing.

Old people are sometimes startled when someone addresses them. They've already gotten used to being invisible to those around them. Then they get happy that someone has noticed them.

The elevator arrives from above.

I can tell from the red arrow. If I still remember cor-rectly from my sterilization, the cafeteria's in the basement.

The elevator doors pull apart from each other with a loud screech and invite me in. Nobody else in the elevator. Good. I push the button marked B.

Cafeteria is written next to the B. I use the ride down to hoist up my toga with the hand holding my money and pull out my homemade tampon with the other hand. Bloody and slimy as it is, I'll put it near the panel of buttons, the most scrutinized place in this moving crate. Just below the button panel is a bar you can pull down, like a handrail. I yank the horseshoe-shaped bar down and balance the bloody, sticky lump right in the middle of it. Success. Toga down as if nothing's happened. The doors open and two men are standing there. Perfect. Looks like a father and son. None of the important things in life are discussed much in this family, either. I look at both of their faces. The father is ill. His face is yellowish gray and he's wearing a bathrobe. Lung cancer? The son must be here visiting. I greet them, beam-ing with joy. "Good day, gentlemen."

And walk out with perfect posture. It takes a minute. The men have gotten in. The curtains close. I let myself slump back into my bent-over posture and hear from the elevator a weak, old voice, revolted: "What is that? Oh my God."

There's no way they'll clean it up themselves. They'll never figure out that it's just harmless menstrual blood. It looks like something that fell out of a wound. You can't even recognize that it's gauze. Soaked with blood as it is. It could even be a piece of flesh. Human flesh. These days everybody's afraid to come in contact with blood. They'll tell someone on the floor where they get out. The father will hold the doors open to keep my bloody clump from traveling onward. The son will have to go find a nurse on the hall. The nurse will then have to find a rubber glove and a garbage bag so she can remove the clump. And eventually a wet cloth to wash off the dirty grab-bar.

She'll thank the father and son. Showing such civil courage in the cause of hygiene. Then my masterpiece will end up with the medical waste.

I've arrived at the cafeteria. The bills have in the meantime been passed between both hands and smeared with blood. The finger that was inside me also clearly has blood under the fingernail. Blood turns brown when it's exposed to the air. So it looks more like crap or dirt. So my period-hands now look more like the dirty hands of a kid on a playground. I'll nibble it all out from under my nails later. Cleaning your nails with your teeth in public looks as if you're chewing your nails—and I hate that. Chewing your nails is considered by almost everyone to be a sign of psychological weakness. Insecurity. Nervousness. It's something that belongs behind closed doors. Kill or be killed. Coffee, please. As a reward for the long trip here, I'll treat myself to caramel flavor.

I pay with a bloody bill. Pleased that this bill will sooner or later make the rounds. First it'll be clamped under the spring-loaded plastic clip in the drawer of the cash register. Until it's handed out as change. Then it'll wander into a sick person's wallet and, later, when that person is released, will be carried out into the world. Whenever I get a bill with blood on it, my first thought is always of a nose bloodied from snorting too much coke. A bit of blood often gets on the part of the rolled-up bill that was stuck into the nose. Bit of snot, bit of blood. Maybe I should rethink that. There's more than one way to get blood on a bill. I take my coffee and my change to an empty table in the cafeteria. I've done it. I'm sitting here like a normal hospital patient drinking a cup of coffee. I have a long journey behind me, and I've disturbed at least three people through hygienic transgressions. A good day.

While I'm drinking my coffee, I need to figure out how I can manage to stay in the hospital for a while longer. Somehow I need to inflict another injury on myself or else reopen the one I already have. But how, without it looking purposeful? So my parents don't get suspicious. Not to mention the doctors. The cafeteria is slowly beginning to fill up. It's teatime. Most of the people here want to get out of the hospital as fast as they can. I want to stay as long as possible. I think the only other people who want to stay in the hospital as long as possible are the homeless. In our town there's Blind Willy. I don't know why everybody calls him that, because he's not blind. At least not when I talk to him. I always want to give him something. Mom says if you give them money they just drink themselves to death that much faster. Or they buy drugs. She has no clue. Whenever I was downtown without her I would talk to him and get close to his face so I could smell his breath. Not a whiff of alcohol. She was wrong on that count. And I asked him about the drugs. He just laughed and shook his head. I believe him. So I stole some money out of mom's purse and put it aside. Then the next time I went into town without mom, I gave it to him and told him it was from my mother. She sends her best. I told him he shouldn't ever thank her, though, because she wouldn't want it to seem as if she were seeking a public show of gratitude. He took her for a generous, humble lady rather than a hypocritical Christian. I also stole a sleeping bag, food, and clothing for Willy from home. As far as he knows, it all came from her. Whenever I walked past him with mom, he and I would look at each other briefly and then lower our gazes with knowing smiles.

Willy is probably happy when there's something wrong with his leg or something so he can spend a night in the hospital.

If I'm to have any chance at all of bringing my parents together, I need a lot more time here. I would pay to have any of these people's diseases. But there's no point in even thinking about that. It won't work. Just like trading breasts with my friend Corinna. She has big breasts with soft, light-pink nipples. I have small breasts with hard, maroon nipples. Whenever I see the way her tits bulge out of a T-shirt, I want to trade. I picture the two of us going to the plastic surgeon and each having our breasts removed and then reattached on the other. I always have to convince myself to stop thinking about it because no matter how badly I want it, it'll never work. It breaks my heart that something like that isn't yet possible. And besides, I'd still have to ask Corinna whether she was cool with it. I couldn't do it without her consent. Or maybe I could. But then I'd definitely lose her as a friend. But I can't do it anyway because it's simply impossible. Get it through your head, Helen! Quit torturing yourself by letting your mind wander down these hopeless cul-de-sacs. It's just as much of a waste of mental energy to think about how much you would pay the people here for their various diseases. It won't work.

This is no place to figure out a plan to extend my stay here. I'm just too distracted by the other inmates.

I also notice that the coffee is having its usual effect on me. My innards are starting to gurgle and rumble. I react to a cup of coffee the same way a native in the rain forest would to the first cup of his life. With symptoms of poisoning. Half a cup of coffee in the top, diarrhea immediately out the bottom. I did a coffee piss-test once. My dad taught me how. When you get up in the morning, you usually have to pee because your bladder has stored it up all night. So when you've pissed yourself empty in the morning, you can pretty much assume there's basically no more pee left in your body. Now, if you drink a cup of coffee with breakfast, your body feels so poisoned that it leeches water from itself in order to wash out the poisonous drink as quickly as possible. You have to go to the bathroom as soon as you finish drinking it and piss out more fluid than you just drank in the form of coffee. I've confirmed this by using the coffee mug as a measuring cup. The pee always sloshes over the edge. So to the delight of my father I proved the dehydrating effect of coffee. My mother wasn't pleased, though, because she doesn't think urine belongs in a coffee mug.

I've got to get back to my room. It's go time. My body is starting to fend off the coffee. There's no way I can use a public toilet down here in case I have to crap. I'm scared of that and need peace and quiet. It might also hurt so badly that I have to scream. This isn't the place for that. That's something I'd want to do on my own. Quick, back to my room. Though it's not like me, I don't take my cup to the cart at the exit for dirty dishes—despite the fact that I want to be a model patient. In an emergency you can leave your

cup. Just stand up and make your way slowly to the elevator. And cinch closed what's left of your sphincter muscle
so nothing ends up in the sheet.

Just in the nick of time I remember that I got rid of
my do-it-yourself tampon for the sake of a prank. I'm squeez-
ing everything down there together as best as I can. In the
front, too. A Roman with a bloody toga walking around the
cafeteria. That would create quite a sensation. Don't want
that. Thanks to my pussy's good musculature, I can hold blood
in for quite a while. Then, when I sit on the toilet and relax
my muscles, it all sloshes out of me at once. At the elevator
I tell myself I've already made it halfway. Once I get on the
elevator I'll just have to stand still and then when I get out
on my floor I'll only have to make it the same distance I did
from the chair in the cafeteria to the elevator.

Ding. It's here. I immediately look for what I left behind. Nothing. As I thought. Tampon gone. Not even a hint
of a drop of blood. Drops of blood have a very short half-
life in a hospital. When the doors have closed, I stick the
tip of my pointer finger into my blood-holder and dab an
oval of blood—like a potato print in school—in the exact
spot where my goods were. They won't catch me. The doors
open. I walk to my room so fast it hurts. The pressure is
building. I'm worried about what's going to come out and
how. I stand over the toilet bowl with my legs spread apart,
pull the gauze plug out of my ass and let nature take its

course. I don't need to paint a picture, but it takes a while, hurts a lot, bleeds heavily, and now I've done it. The thing everyone here is waiting for me to do. But they're never going to know. I make a new plug out of toilet paper. Air this place out. The telltale scent has got to go. First I turn on the shower full blast. Somebody once told me the water pulls bad smells down the drain. I leave the door to the bathroom open and walk even more buckled over than before to the window next to my bed and open it as wide as it goes. I walk gingerly because of the postfecal pain. But I'm in a hurry. Back to the bathroom door. I open and close the door, fanning the air in the direction of the window. I don't smell anything anymore. But that will need to be confirmed. I go back out into the hall and close the door to my room. I take a few deep breaths in and out until I have only fresh, stench-free air in my nose and lungs. Then I go back in, just as any nurse would, and sniff. The smell is gone. Everything's clean. No evidence. Mission accomplished. I turn off the water and make a new homemade tampon to handle my menstrual blood. Done. Calm. What should I do now? I'll lie down and close my eyes. Let's simmer down—or at least get worked up over something else.

I'm thinking of Robin. I undress him. Lay him totally naked on my hospital bed and lick him from his tailbone all the way up his backbone to his neck. He has a lot of dark moles. Maybe he should visit the skin doctor. It would be a shame if he died of skin cancer. He's a nurse, after all. A nurse shouldn't die of something overlooked. A nurse should get run over by a car or kill himself because he's fallen hopelessly in love with someone. Like me, for instance. I lick each vertebrae all the way back down. To his butt crack. I spread his cheeks apart and lick his asshole. At first just in a circle. Then I make my tongue pointed and stiff and bore into his tightly closed sphincter. My left hand makes its way underneath to his cock. It's so hard it's like a stone column wrapped in warm skin. I shove my tongue deeper into his ass and hold my closed hand against his bell-end. I want him to come so hard into my pressed-together fingers that it streams out the other side. Which is exactly what he does. There's nothing else he can do. I don't let go of the tip of his cock. Hold it tight. I open my eyes again. He's a pig, this

Robin. I have to laugh. I love my emergency sex fantasy. I don't need TV to entertain myself.

A knock at the door. With my luck it'll be Robin and he'll instantly figure out what I was just picturing. Nope. A female nurse. She asks whether I've had a bowel movement.

"No, have you?"

The nurse gives a pained smile and leaves.

Helen, you wanted to be a good patient. Yes, but with the constant questions and the phrase "bowel movement" it's tough to be nice. And now. I'll combine two things in one trip. I'll pee and go out into the hall to get mineral water for my hidden avocado pits. I slide out of bed backward, as always, dropping my feet to the ground until they are both solidly planted. Twinges of pain are beginning. The anesthesiologist warned me about this. It's on the way. I waddle to the washroom, lift my hospital gown and piss standing up, just the way an ass patient is supposed to. No need to flush. Nobody else is going to use it but me. Drives hygiene-freaks nuts. From the sink I grab the glass you're supposed to use to rinse your mouth out after you brush your teeth and fill it to overflowing with water. Dad taught me that water can stay in a glass even if you fill it above the rim— because of the surface tension or something like that. I can't remember exactly anymore. I'll ask him again when he shows up. Now I've already got a conversation topic prepared. You need to do that with him. And this is just the sort of thing he loves to talk about for long periods of time. There won't be any embarrassing pauses in the conversation.

I drink the entire glass in one go. Nice change. Still water instead of sparkling.

I leave my gown gathered and tied in front. I'd be ashamed to have any of my schoolmates visit me, but I don't care if everyone here sees me undressed all day long. They've seen it all here, that's for sure. From the bathroom I don't go back to bed but out into the hall. I stand there for a minute and look around. On the way to the cafeteria I saw a little seating area for visitors. Where you can make tea or get coffee out of a big urn. And right there was a tower of stacked water-bottle crates. Surely they're self-serve. I'll try it out. Because to fill the pit glasses I need more than one bottle. And the nurses only bring a new bottle once the last one is empty. It's too indulgent for me to make a nurse take several trips back and forth. I head for the seating area. There's a family sitting there speaking to each other very quietly. The nurses should follow their lead. One of the men in the group is wearing pajamas and a bathrobe. That signals to me that he's the ass patient of the bunch. I don't feel like saying hello. I take three bottles out of the top crate and head back. I can hear that my rearview has created a stir among the family. Have a ball. I walk as quickly as I can back to my protected cave.

I squeeze into the far corner between the windowsill and the bed without letting my ass brush up against anything. Back to where I've hidden my avocado greenhouse with the Bible. Shielded from the view of the doctors and nurses and from Robin. Although Robin's allowed to see them. I'll show him at some point. He's already seen a lot. Come to think of it, he could take some pictures of the current condition of my ass.

I lift up the Bible carefully and refill the glasses. In the sun here on the windowsill the water evaporates pretty fast. Don't think you have nothing to do, Helen. There are living things depending on you. You can do a better job keeping them watered. Some of the pits are already out of the water, and here you are saying you're bored. Tsk, tsk. They all look to be doing okay, though. Sometimes one here or there will start to mold and I have to part with it despite all the effort I've put in. The roots aren't yet sticking out of most of them. But one has started to split, and another has a root growing out of the bottom. Things are going well with my pits. All healthy. I put the Bible back and shield them from view again.

I think I'd like to stand here for a minute. The room looks completely different from here.

Up to now I've mostly looked out from the bed. From here the room looks bigger. Of course. I'm in the farthest corner. With all my power I push the bed a few inches into the room and then let myself slide down into the corner until my ass touches the floor and my legs are bent so much that my knees touch my breastbone. I feel the cold linoleum on my peach and ass cheeks. I don't even know if it is linoleum, but that's what people always say is in a hospital. This position is straining my ass too much. I need to straighten out my legs under the bed. I can hide here. If I can't see the door, nobody who comes through the door can see my face either. My legs yes. But they'd have to purposefully look under the bed first. Nobody who comes in will have any reason to look under the bed. Everyone will just look at the bed and, if it's empty, think that I'm wandering around somewhere or that I'm on the toilet. I feel between my legs with my hand. I stick two fingers in and use them like tweezers to pull out my home-made tampon. I put it on top of the shoulder-high radiator. The tampon wobbles back and forth unsteadily so I press it down between two ribs of the radiator. I don't want it to fall on me. I don't want to have any bloodstains in strange places on my back or wherever that nobody can explain—and that I can't either because I can't even see them. As soon as I've positioned the tampon securely—it's a bit sticky now, too, which helps—I take my middle finger and put the tip of the nail directly on my snail tail. I press on it with the edge of the nail. That must make an indentation. Nobody sees it though. It's the fastest way to get wet. My pussy immediately begins to drip with slime. One hand is busy with the snail tail—I alternately press on it and rub it; I need two fingers of the other hand to shove into my pussy. I spread the two fingers apart inside my pussy and make a twisting motion. Normally, as I get more and more into it I stick my pussy fingers in my ass. That's not going to happen, though. The ass is fresh from surgery and already occupied by a plug. I could try to feel that, though. I move the pussy fingers inside me toward the back. It feels like a very thin dividing wall between pussy and ass. I can feel the plug. Even though I'm in the pussy. I know this feeling. But not from a plug, of course. From shit. It's often lined up at the exit before it's allowed to leave. And if you're in the pussy you can feel the log of crap through the thin dividing wall. I wonder if men have ever felt one in me when we were hooking up?

They would never say anything about it anyway. It wouldn't seem like the most appropriate thing to say right before you stuck your cock in someone.

"Hey, wow, you know what I just felt inside you?" Not likely.

I also like to feel the sphincter work from my pussy. I tighten it, cinch my ass closed, and feel it from inside.

There's a cow on the grass, hallelujah. Opens and closes its ass, hallelujah.

Now I want to feel the front wall of my pussy. The back wall has been sufficiently investigated.

By turning my fingers all the way around—a feeling that really turns me on, I love quick twisting motions inside me—I'm touching the front wall of my pussy, directly behind the pubic bone. Here the pussy feels like a washboard. You say a muscular man has a washboard stomach, too. But that's not a very good comparison. The front wall of the pussy feels like an actual washboard, in miniature. Like a cheese grater. That's it! A cheese grater. It's a hard landscape of bumps like that—like the top of your mouth but with bigger bumps. The way the roof of a lion's mouth looks when it yawns and you can see inside it. That's exactly how the front wall of the pussy feels. When I press hard against it, it feels as if I'm going to piss all over my hand and I usually come immediately. When I come that way, a fluid often shoots out, too, like sperm. I don't think there's much difference between men and women. But that's not how I want to come today.

I have to stop exploring the inside of my body.

I need both hands now. I rub my dewlaps really hard with both pointer fingers. Almost there, almost there. One hand works its way up. I want to brace myself on the windowsill. When I come I like to hold onto something sturdy.

I come fast. Usually.

Suddenly there's water all over me. It's ice cold. No way I can come now. I've knocked over one of the avocado glasses and the water's spilled onto my head and run down my chest.

I look down at my body. My hospital gown is see-through now from the water. My maroon nipples show and they're sticking out because they're cold. If there's a wet T-shirt contest at the hospital today I'll win.

But first I'll finish my mission. I press my middle finger against my little snail tail again and make tiny circular motions with it. This gets me back in the mood again and starts to warm me up from below. But that feeling that spreads across your pelvis just won't come back because of the chill of the water. It's just not going to work. I can't even quietly give myself a handjob hidden under the bed in my own hospital room. Usually the easiest task.

Sorry, Helen.

I want to get back up. Just as I've lifted my ass a few inches above the puddle, there's a knock at the door. As always, the door opens simultaneously. Nobody here waits for a "come in."

They must already have their right hand on the door handle as they knock with the left. As they are knocking they open the door.

They keep catching me with my hand on my pussy. I've given up trying to quickly pull my hand away. It's even more obvious than just leaving your hand there.

There are no secrets in the hospital. I've given up on secrets. Otherwise I'd have to hate all these intruders too much.

I can see feet and a handle with a big mop attached to the bottom of it. The cleaning woman is making her rounds.

I don't want her to see me. The mop snakes softly around the floor. An animal that's coming in my direction. I hold my breath. People always think their breathing will give them away. But that's stupid. I normally breathe very quietly. She starts at the door and works her way past the front of the wardrobe, toward the bed. Snaking lines. Back and forth. I see her corral some crumbs and push them around. I notice some hair, long and dark, probably mine—who else's?—just before the wet mop gets them. The mop also pushes dust bunnies. Those things that form when hair or splinters or lint tangle themselves up into little bird's nests. She slowly mops until she reaches the metal nightstand. She'll probably slide the mop under the bed; I grimace as I pull my legs up. She does. Good prediction. I see the handle lean on the bed now. She's stopped mopping. There's a metallic banging. She's opened the chrome trash can on the nightstand.

"Bah."

What does that mean? Bah. She must have seen the towels in the trash can. She shouldn't look so closely. There's nothing else I could have done with them.

I hear the drawer of my nightstand open.

No way. What is she doing in there? Get out! There's nothing to clean in there—only something to steal. Money.

The drawer closes again. I'll look to see what's missing. That was a favorite game for us at home. In a wardrobe or on a table, my father would make us look away and then remove something. Then we'd have to figure out what was gone.

I'm good at it. Just you wait . . .

I look at the newly washed, still wet, glistening floor. She leaves footprints on the freshly mopped surface. Right. Of course. She did it wrong. No way. She started at the door and then tracked dirt right back over everything. When she leaves, everything will look dirtier than before. Maybe she's new. I could tell her how to do it, just a little tip. I see her leaving footprints as she walks toward the door. But she pulls the mop behind her, snaking it back and forth. Footprints gone. All upset for no reason, Helen. Interesting technique.

She pulls the door closed behind her. I've already started to hoist myself up onto the bed.

As fast as the plug in my ass allows me, I circle the foot of the bed and go around to the metal nightstand.

I open the drawer and look and look. I realize nothing's missing. It's a great relief. It would be horrible if the cleaning woman were stealing from hospital patients. I would have to have registered a complaint and she would have probably lost her job.

So why did she open the drawer?

Maybe she just wants to see what people have. Maybe it's a tick or a fetish of hers. You could also call it a hobby, I guess.

I'll never know. Even if I asked her, I know she wouldn't answer honestly. That's just the way people are.

I would divulge my fetishes. But nobody asks me. Nobody thinks to.

I scrutinize the drawer once more. Think. But it's true. Not even the smallest thing is missing.

I get back into bed and ring the emergency call button. A nurse comes in surprisingly quickly. I tell her the cleaning woman has just been here but that she didn't notice a big puddle of water in the corner. I lie and say I spilled a glass of water. Very believable, Helen. Sometimes you're strange. How is that supposed to have happened? Unless you purposefully dumped a full glass over there. The nurse doesn't ask any questions or show any signs of suspicion—at least I don't notice it if she does. And she calls the cleaning woman back into the room.

She comes in and opens her eyes wide with surprise because I'm suddenly there in bed. I hold the sheet in front of my wet, see-through shirt.

The nurse points behind the bed and explains in a nasty tone of voice—like a command, in exaggeratedly simple words—what the cleaning woman needs to do.

The nurse disappears through the magic door. Without asking, the cleaning woman shoves me and my sickbed away from the windowsill. It's a nice feeling, like being on a flying carpet. Or rather, what you imagine it might be like on a flying carpet—they don't exist, right? But I don't let myself show the pleasure of the sensation. You're supposed to be upset when someone just shoves you around in your bed as if you were an object or you were in a coma.

Unlike when I'm in a car, I'm very sensitive to turns and stops here. When she suddenly stops the bed after the two-yard drive, I nearly fall out. I let out a high-pitched cry. I always do that when something happens to me, good or bad. I scream loud. If I stumble over something I let out a major scream. Let it all out, that's my motto—otherwise you'll get cancer. I'm very loud in bed, too. I'm in bed now, of course. But this is different.

As I scream I can see the corner of the cleaning woman's mouth twitch—upward, not downward. Ha. She's taking pleasure in my misfortune. That pisses me off. I promise myself that if she's ever in the hospital, lying there helpless, I'll push her around like Aladdin and when she screams I'll let the corner of my mouth turn up like that so she can see how it feels. I swear I will. Helen. Very impressive.

While I'm dreaming up my *One Thousand and One Nights* revenge fantasy, she's already set about cleaning up the puddle. She's quick with the mop. She keeps moving it over the same area in the form of the sign for infinity we learned in school, soaking up the water. A figure eight. Again and again.

Something suddenly occurs to me. My lungs, or my heart, or something else in there, makes a sickening jump. My gaze wanders up the radiator and there is my bloody wad. Oh no. Forgot about that. She hasn't noticed it up to this point. The slots of the built-in radiator are probably not a main area of focus for her duties. I might get lucky and she'll just swish around in the corner and never raise her eyes above the level of the mop. I try to calm my fears with this possibility. I really hope she doesn't see the bloody wad. Funny how things can sometimes be excruciatingly embarrassing and other times perfectly okay. If she said "Bah" to the contents of my trash can, how will she react if she spots that? Please, don't let that happen.

I say thanks and ask her to push me back toward the windowsill even though she still hasn't stopped mopping up. She can just push me back like a patient in a wheelchair and then leave.

She leans the mop against the wall at the foot end of the bed. She grabs the rail that runs around my bed with her strong hands and rams me and the bed far too hard toward the window. Bam. It smacks into the wall and I scream again.

Yep, all her resentment over cleaning up after filthy patients packed into one motion.

She grabs the mop and heads out. Just before she closes the door behind her she says, "Funny—if the glass fell over, why is it sitting there full?"

My heart skips a beat again.

I look over at the metal nightstand and see the full glass of water. I'm terrible at making up fake explanations.

The time between when I hit upon the idea to masturbate in the corner and this moment feels like hours. Very stressful and not at all relaxing as I had imagined it would be.

I toss the bloody clump into the chrome trash can.

Don't be disappointed. Your next self-fuck will be better, Helen.

I look around the room. Have you forgotten anything else you don't want to reveal to others?

Nope, everything's back in place, where it all belongs.

I just need to get out of this wet gown. Undress first and then ring the buzzer, or ring first and then undress? Helen? You wouldn't be Helen if you were to ring first.

I take off my top and cover my breasts with the sheet. It feels nice. The crisp sheet against the skin of my chest. I wonder if the sheets are put through a heated roller press? Is that what it's called? I always read the signs of laundromats as I go past. I know this cool feeling on my chest from home. Mom places a lot of importance on perfect linens. Only for me to sully them.

Now I ring the buzzer.

Please. Let it be Robin instead of somebody else.

Sometimes I get lucky. Robin comes in.

"What's up, Helen?"

"Can I have a fresh gown?"

I hand him the wet one in a bundle and make sure the sheet slips down enough so he can catch a glimpse of both nipples.

"Of course. What happened? There wasn't bleeding, was there?"

He's worried about me. Amazing. After all he's had to listen to from me. And to look at. I can't believe it.

"No, no. No bleeding. I would tell you immediately if that happened. I tried to masturbate under the bed and I accidentally knocked over a glass of water and it spilled on me. Everything got wet."

He laughs and shakes his head.

"Very funny, Helen. I get it. You don't want to tell me what happened. I'll get you a new one anyway. Be right back."

In the short time it takes Robin to go to some cabinet somewhere and find a new tree-top angel outfit, I get bored and lonely. What to do? With one hand I push down the pedal that opens the chrome trash can on my nightstand and with the other I reach in. The homemade tampon's no longer red from fresh blood but brown from old blood. I open the Tupperware container on the other side of the bed and put the lump of bloody toilet paper in with the unused hygiene articles. I hope my bacteria multiplies and spreads in there and—invisible, as bacteria is—gets all over the gauze bandages and pads. The box is steamed up from sitting in the sun. For my purposes it has perfect petri-dish conditions. I'll have to remember to get rid of it at some point. When I'm released, the next patient will be able to further my experiment by proving to me and the world that nothing bad happens when you use bandages with other people's bacteria on them to stop the bleeding in your open wound. I'll keep track of the experiment as a candy striper, knocking on the door, daily, and opening it at the same time, catching ass patients masturbating on the floor. You get to know people fast that way.

Robin comes back in.

He hands me the gown, smiling. I drop the sheet into my lap. I act as if it's nothing to me for him to see me completely topless. I strike up a conversation, more to keep myself from losing my cool. I pull the gown over my arms and ask him to tie it in the back. He ties a little bow in back and says he has to get back to work. But he also says "unfortunately."

He's gone for a while and then there's a knock at the door again. He must have forgotten something. Or he wants to tell me something. Please.

Nope. It's my father. Surprise visit. I'll never get the two of them in the room together at this rate. My parents, that is. If they come and go as they please without listening to the visit coordinator. My father has something strange in his hand.

"Hello, my daughter. How are you doing?"

"Hi, dad. Have you had a bowel movement?"

"You're outrageous," he says, laughing. I'm sure he can figure out why I'm asking him this question.

I put out my hand the way I always do when dad's supposed to have something for me. He puts whatever it is he's brought in my hand. Some strange thing made out of clear plastic.

"Is it a balloon? A gray balloon? Thanks, dad. I'm sure it'll help me get well soon."

"Open it. You've jumped the gun, my daughter."

It looks like an uninflated neck pillow, but instead of being horseshoe-shaped it's round, like a life preserver for really small people.

"Stumped? It's a hemorrhoid pillow. So you can sit without it hurting. The sore part goes in the middle of the ring so it floats in the air. If it's not touching anything, it can't cause you pain."

"Oh, thanks, dad." He's obviously spent a lot of time thinking about me in pain and wondering what he could do to help. My father has feelings. And feelings for me. Nice.

"Where can you buy such a thing, dad?"

"One of those stores that sells surgical equipment and health-care products and whatnot."

"Aren't they called medical-supply stores?"

"Yes, that sounds right. A medical-supply store."

This is already a long conversation for us, given the circumstances.

I rip open the plastic wrap. And start to blow up the pillow ring. I guess lying around and imagining having sex with the nurse doesn't make your lungs any stronger. After a few puffs I'm seeing stars in front of my eyes. I hand the pillow over to dad so he can finish the job.

I left an extra gob of spit on the inflation valve on my last puff. Dad puts it in his mouth without wiping it off. That's the precursor to a French kiss. Wouldn't it be considered that? I can definitely imagine having sex with my father. Years ago, when I was young and my parents still lived together, they would always walk naked to the bathroom in the morning. A thick club grew from my father's groin. Even as a kid I was fascinated by it. They thought I didn't notice. But I did. And how.

I didn't know about morning wood back then. I only learned about that much later. Even after I was fucking boys I still thought for a long time that morning erection was because of me. It was a big disappointment to learn men have them to keep their piss from running out. Major disappointment.

I watch my father blowing up the pillow and have to laugh. The way he's concentrating so seriously and putting his all into it reminds me of earlier times. We were on vacation at the beach and he blew up a bunch of huge inflatable animals and air mattresses for me and my brother—he was completely exhausted. That's fatherly love. He was also supposed to put sunscreen on my back to protect me from getting burned. I rubbed it onto all the places I could reach by myself. I never got burned in those places. But my back, which my father was responsible for, was always burned. Sometimes really badly. When I would look at my sunburned back in the mirror in the evening, I could tell dad had done a lazy job. There was a big white question mark on my back, and everything else was fiery red. He had obviously squirted a blob of sunscreen into his hand and just made a quick arc across my back and called it a day. I always thought it took him far too little time. So much for fatherly love. Maybe he was just too depleted from blowing up all those inflatable toys to be able to properly cover me with sunscreen. Maybe it was just too much to ask for. Probably. I do that all the time. Ask for too much.

He notices me smiling.

"What?" He doesn't even take his mouth off the valve.

He's thoroughly mixed his spit with mine. Does he find that as interesting as I do? Does he think about such things, too? If you don't ask, you never find out the answer. And I'll never ask.

"Nothing. Thanks for the hemorrhoid pillow and for blowing it up, dad."

The door opens. Now they've stopped knocking altogether.

It's a new nurse. How many are there here?

I already know what she wants.

"No, I haven't had a bowel movement."

"That's not what I wanted. I just wanted to change the plastic bag in your trash can. You produce such a steady stream of used gauze pads."

"Well my ass is producing a steady stream of blood and ass piss."

The nurse—Valerie according to her nametag—and my father just stare at me in shock. Go ahead, stare. So what? All the belittling by the nursing staff is slowly starting to get on my nerves.

The nurse quickly pulls the plastic bag out of the chrome trash can, puts a knot in the top of it, snaps open a new one like a windsock, and puts it into the trash can. She watches my father continue inflating the pillow.

She lets the top of the trash can close loudly and says, as she's walking out, "If that pillow is supposed to be for the patient, I'd advise against it. It'll tear everything open again if she sits in it. It's not for people who have had surgery."

My father gets up and puts the pillow in my wardrobe. He seems sad that he's given me something harmful.

Now what? He says he has to get going soon. Needs to get to work. What does he even do?

With certain things, if you don't ask about them soon enough you can never ask about them.

Because I've been hanging around boys for so long, I never paid any attention to what my father did. I can only guess from what others used to say at family meals that it has something to do with research and science.

I promise myself that when I get out of the hospital, which shouldn't be too long from now, I'll look through the things in my father's secret cabinet and figure out what he does.

"Okay, dad. Say hi to all your coworkers from a stranger."

"What coworkers?" he says softly as he walks out the door.

My dad has a whole lot of gray and silver hair now. He'll die soon. That means I'll have to part with him soon. It's best if I get used to the idea now so it hurts less when it happens. I'll make a mental note of it in my forgetful, sievelike brain: make peace with the fact that you have to say good-bye to dad. When it actually comes to pass, everyone will wonder how I manage to come to grips with it so well. Winning the battle of mourning by advanced preparation.

One thing my father's short visit accomplished is that I now know how I can remain in the hospital longer. All I have to do is sit on the ring pillow with a lot of pressure and my wound will rip open again. That's what the huffy Valerie promised would happen. I just can't get caught. I take a pain-killer. A little numbness is something I'm definitely going to want.

Using my proven method I turn onto my stomach, shimmy down off the bed, and, hunched over with pain, walk over to the wardrobe. I open the doors my father closed. Down on the bottom is the would-be culprit. The normal squatting down by bending my legs won't work. Hurts too much. I'll have to figure out another way to reach down and pick it up. I keep my legs straight and bend at the waist. Keep my back straight, too. I look like an upside-down L now. I can just barely reach the ring with my hand. Success. Raise my back upright again. And retrace my steps. Back beside the bed, I put the ring down near the edge of the mattress so I can sit directly on it from a standing position. I turn my ass to the bed and sit myself down like a bird on a nest. I wiggle around on my ass. A little this way, a little that way, it's not difficult. With the movement, the skin of the wound really strains. I stand up and feel around back there with my hand. I look at my hand. No blood! You promised too much, Valerie.

What now? It was a good plan to reopen the wound. Won't work with the pillow. I'll have to find something else to rip open my ass. Concentrate, Helen. You don't have a lot of time. You know how often the door opens and witnesses come in. I look at all the available objects in the room. Metal nightstand: useless. Bottle of water on the nightstand: you could stick it in, but I don't think you'd be able to hurt yourself with it the way I need to. Television: too high. The spoons on the table: too harmless. Granola bowl: you can't do anything with that. My gaze falls on the bed. There. That's it. The brakes on the bed's rollers. The wheels are big and metal with a rubber coating. They're equipped with some sort of foot brakes, operated by a metal pedal that sticks out. You've got the job, pedal. I go as fast as I can to the end of the bed. I line my back up with it and slide awkwardly down, letting my ass land on the pedal. Now I sit on it. I wiggle back and forth. I have to scream with pain and put both of my hands over my mouth. If this doesn't work I don't know what I'm going to do. I can feel the pedal penetrating the wound. Pressing down hard I make it bore in deeper. This is going to have to do. Valiant Helen. Well done. I'm crying and shaking with pain. It must have worked. My test hand makes its way down and wipes around. I look. My entire palm is covered with fresh, red blood. I need to lie down fast or I'm going to faint right here. That would ruin the whole exercise. I need to be found lying in bed so I can pretend it just happened to me as I was lying there. I lie down.

It hurts like hell. I'm still holding my mouth shut. Tears stream down my face. Should I call somebody now or wait so the wound makes more of an impression? I'll wait. I can manage. Be sure to wipe off the brake pedal, Helen, and get rid of the evidence. The hemorrhoid pillow I hide under the covers. I can take care of that later. More and more blood is gushing out. I reach back with my hand again and this time it's even more covered with blood than the first time. The feeling in my crotch and down my legs is just like when you wet yourself as a kid. When body-temperature liquid is

running down you, the first innocent thought is of piss—
since that's what it's usually been in past experience. I lie
in a pool of my own blood and cry. I open my eyes and see
an upside-down bottle cap from the mineral water on my
nightstand. I take it in my hand and try to catch my tears.
I can distract myself from the horrible pain with this challenge, and maybe I'll find a use for the tears later. I almost
never cry. But now its just spewing out of me. Tears up top,
blood down below.

I hold the bottle cap up near my tear ducts and after a
few seconds look to see what I've managed to collect. At
least the bottom of the cap is wet. Helen, you've fooled
around long enough. I push the emergency buzzer. As I'm
waiting for someone to come, I hide the bottle cap at the
back of my nightstand behind everything else. So none of
these idiots knock it over. There's a lot of pain in that little
vessel.

I think it's high time somebody showed up. I am, after
all, losing a lot of blood. Regardless of whether I did it to
myself or it just happened. They have to help me stop the
bleeding now. So much has gushed out of me that it's dripping onto the floor. How is that possible? Shouldn't the
bed soak it up? I know. Because of the plastic lining. The
blood is pooling beneath me and not soaking in to the mattress. It's trickling past me onto the floor. I lie in bed and
look at my blood on the floor. There's more and more.

Interesting view. It's beginning to look like a butcher's shop in here. Only the butcher's floor slopes into a runoff channel so the blood can drain. They should think about doing that here in the proctology unit. Though not many patients do to themselves what I've just done to my ass. Forget putting a drainage channel in the floor. Bad idea. I push the buzzer again. Three times, one after the other. I can hear out on the hall that it doesn't help. Pushing three times still only creates a single tone in the nurses' station. They don't want to be driven crazy by the patients. Though they could use a more clever system for communications between the patients and staff. One buzz: I need a little more butter for my whole-grain bread. Two buzzes: please bring a flower vase with water. Three buzzes: help, blood is gushing out of my ass so fast that I hardly have enough left in my brain to think straight and I'm stuck here thinking up stupid ways to improve the hospital.

I can see the blood-smeared brake pedal. I've got to wipe that clean or I'm going to get it. I stand up quickly and nearly slip over in my own blood. I brace myself on the bed and go slowly toward the foot of it. The blood splashes up between my toes and onto my foot. I have to be careful not to hydroplane on the blood. I squat down and wipe the pedal with a corner of my gown. Evidence gone. Well. At least the evidence on the brake pedal. Squatting hurts. Walking hurts. I'm about to collapse. Come on, Helen, you can make it into bed. Lie down, little one. Made it. I press both hands to my face.

I wait an eternity. You always have to wait. I could also go to them and cause a big commotion by leaving a trail of blood down the hallway. I'll restrain myself from doing that.

I'm getting dizzy. It smells like blood in here. A lot of blood. Shall I use the time to clean up a little? After all, I want to be the best patient they've ever had. But maybe that's asking too much of myself. I don't need to tidy up right now.

Knock. The door opens. Robin. Good. He can do it. Do what exactly, Helen? Whatever. I'm going downhill fast.

I explain right away: "I don't know what happened. I think I must have moved in an odd way and all of a sudden the blood started to gush. What should we do now?"

Robin's eyes open wide. He says he's going to call the doctor right away.

He comes up to me. Didn't he say he was going to call the doctor?

He says I look pale. He's stepped in the pooled blood and as he goes out he tracks bloody footprints all over the room.

I think to myself afterward: be careful you don't hydroplane on the blood. I hold both hands on the bleeding, trying to slow it. My hands fill with blood. What a waste. Don't some people have too little blood? Or is it that they have diseased blood? How should I know?

Anemic. That's what it is. There are people they describe as anemic. You will be, too, soon, Helen, if you keep this up.

The anesthesiologist comes in. He asks if I've eaten anything. I have. I had a lot of granola for breakfast. He finds this a shame. Why?

"Because then you can't have general anesthesia. There's too much risk you'll vomit in your sleep and suffocate. An epidural is the only possibility."

He runs out and returns with a form and needles and some other stuff.

That's what pregnant women get, pregnant women who can't manage a normal birth. Cowardly mothers. Ones who want a natural birth but with no pain, thanks. I've heard about it from my mother.

I have to sign something. I'm not sure what it is because I wasn't listening. I trust him. It definitely makes me nervous that this otherwise calm man is running around. I begin to worry about myself. He seems to be in a major hurry.

They think I've lost too much blood too fast. Once I realize they think the same thing I do, I'm sick with fear—afraid I may die as a result of my plan to get my parents back together. That wasn't part of the plan.

He says I need to sit up, bend forward, and arch my

back like a cat so he can disinfect my back, insert a thick catheter between my lower vertebrae, and then administer the injection. It doesn't sound good.

I hate anything that gets near my spinal cord. I worry they'll screw up and I'll be permanently paralyzed and never feel anything again during sex. Might as well forget sex then. Everything he says he also simultaneously does. I can feel it as he searches around back there, wipes, inserts, and injects. Sitting in this position increases the pain. It feels as if my ass is ripping open even more.

He says it takes exactly fifteen minutes for everything from the tube to my toes to go numb. It seems like a long time to both him and me. Calculated in liters of blood per minute. He goes out saying he'll be right back. Good. I look at my mobile phone to check the time. Ten past. At twenty-five past I'll be ready for surgery.

Robin comes in and tells me the doctor is getting ready for an emergency operation. That's why he can't come see me. Robin described to him how much blood I had lost. The doctor immediately ordered the emergency surgery.

Emergency operation. Man oh man, that sounds bad. But also important and exciting. As if I'm important. This is a good time to lure my parents here.

I write down my parents' numbers for Robin and ask him to call them during the operation and tell them to come down here.

The anesthesiologist comes in and wants Robin to wheel me to the operating room. I touch my thigh and can feel my hand make contact. Wait. I can still feel everything. They can't operate on me. Not yet. I look at my mobile. Quarter past. Only five minutes have gone by.

They can't be serious. They're not going to wait for the anesthesia to kick in? They're in more of a hurry than I thought. Very unnerving.

Robin pushes me out into the hall. They won't let me take my mobile. Because of all the equipment. What equipment? Are we flying there or something? Whatever.

If I remember correctly, clocks are hanging in all the halls and waiting rooms. Those giant black-and-white train station clocks. Why do they have train station clocks in a hospital? Are they trying to tell us something? I'm not going to let them stick their tools up my ass until fifteen minutes have elapsed. Whether I bleed to death or not. Very defiant, Helen, but stupid. You don't want to die.

It would be the perfect reason for my parents to reunite, though. In their mourning they would drift back toward each other. They wouldn't be able to take comfort in their respective new partners because they know the partners never accepted their stepchildren. If the stepchild dies, the new partner is exposed. Then it'll be clear who won the power struggle and who lost. Great plan, Helen, except you wouldn't be able to experience their reunion. If you die, you won't be watching down from above.

You know that there's no heaven. That we're just highly developed animals. Who, after death, simply rot in the earth and are eaten by worms. There's no possibility of looking down after death at your beloved parental animals. Everything is just devoured. The reputed soul, the memory, every little recollection and bit of love will be turned into worm shit along with the brain. And the eyes. And the pussy. Worms can't tell the difference. They eat synapses as happily as they eat clitorises. For them there's no big picture of what or whom they're eating. Their only concern is that it's tasty.

Back to the time. We pass several clocks but hardly any time is passing. Robin is in a hurry. He bumps into the walls a lot. I can feel the puddle of blood I'm lying in getting deeper.

The depression my ass creates in the mattress has long since overflowed. That I can still feel these things is a bad sign. If I've understood the anesthesiologist correctly, I should feel like a quadriplegic before they start. If I have this much feeling left in my legs, then I must also still have it in my ass.

We've arrived in the prep room. There's a train station clock in here, too. I knew it. Clock-memory contest won. It's eighteen minutes past. I stare at the long hand. Robin explains that we'll be ready to go as soon as the op-erating room's cleared out. Without looking away from the long hand, I tell him: "I'm not a stickler when it comes to tidiness. They don't need to clear the place on my account. I'm happy to have a look at what was going on in there before."

Robin and the anesthesiologist laugh. Typical, Helen. Even in the worst situation you've still got a zinger on the tip of your tongue. It's just so none of them notice how scared I am of them and of having their hands up my ass. I'm very proud of the flexibility of my sphincter muscle during sex, but several adult-male hands is too much for me. Sorry. I just can't see anything good about it.

Now, unfortunately, I know what a blown-out sphinc-ter muscle feels like. And this time they're going to do it without general anesthesia.

These sick pigs. I'm scared. I grab Robin's hand. It was near me, and I hold it tight. He seems used to it. It doesn't surprise him at all.

Every granny probably does the same thing. Most people get really nervous before an operation. Like before a big jour-ney. It really is like a journey. You never know whether you'll return.

A journey of pain. I squeeze Robin's hand so tight that his skin goes white from the pressure. I bore my long nails in so I'll leave a different pattern in his skin than the grannies do. The big motorized doors of the operating room open and a nurse with a surgical mask says, muffled, "Here we go."

Bitch. Panicking, I look at the clock. The long hand jerks down to the four. Tick. Twenty past. The clock hand is still jiggling.

They have to wait five more minutes. No. Don't. I can still feel everything. Please don't start, I think. But don't say. Your own fault, Helen. You wanted to bleed and this is what you got yourself into. I think I might throw up. I don't say that either. If it happens, they'll see it anyway. Nothing matters at this point.

"I'm scared, Robin."

"Me too, for you."

Understood. He loves me. I didn't know. Sometimes it happens that quickly. I put my other hand on his, holding his hand tightly between both of mine. I look him in the eyes and try to smile. Then I let go.

They wheel me in. Lift me onto another bed. The nurses each take one of my legs and loop them in straps hanging from the ceiling. They are fastened at the ankle and then pulled tightly upward. Some kind of pulley. My legs are sticking straight up. Like an extreme version of a gynecological position. So everyone can crawl up my ass. I see long lashes above a surgical mask. Dr. Notz. Robin's gone. Probably too nervous to watch. The anesthesiologist sets up next to my head. He says they have to start now because I'm losing so much blood. He says it only seems as if I can feel everything because there's a miniscule amount of feeling left. In reality, he says, I'll only feel a tiny fraction of what's being done. They've hung a light-green drape between my head and my ass. Obviously so my ass can't see my horror-stricken face.

I ask the anesthesiologist very quietly what exactly they are doing.

He explains to me, as if I am six, that they have to use stitches now, which they normally try to avoid. During my first operation they cut away quite a lot but they were able to leave it open to heal. It's much more pleasant for the patient. Now all of us—and first and foremost me—have had a bit of bad luck. They have to stitch up each and every bloody spot and afterward I'll feel very uncomfortable from the tension. It's really going to pinch. For a long time. And here I was thinking it couldn't get any less comfortable. Oh, Helen, all the things you do for the sake of your parents. Heartwarming. Ha. As the anesthesiologist has been sketching out my painful future for me, I haven't even been paying attention to my ass. Meaning I must be fully numb. I ask the anesthesiologist for the time. Twenty-five minutes past. Feeling gone, to the minute. Very precise with his work. He smiles happily. I do, too.

Suddenly I'm very relaxed, as if nothing is happening.

We can segue into small talk. I ask him inconsequential things that cross my mind. Whether he has to have lunch in the basement cafeteria, too. Whether he has a family. Or a garden. Whether the anesthesia has ever failed to work. Whether it's true that it's more difficult to anesthetize people who take drugs. During the pauses in conversation I picture my parents already waiting together in my empty room, sick with worry over me. Talking about me. About my pain. Nice.

And soon they're done with the stitches. I have feeling in my feet again. I ask the anesthesiologist whether that's possible. He explains that his goal is to numb me just enough. He knows through experience how long these operations last, and numbed me only enough for this amount of time. It looks as if this makes him very proud. Soon I'll feel everything again, including, unfortunately, the pain. For that he gives me a pill. He says it's going to be tough to combat the pain of the tension in my anus with pills. I should prepare myself for serious pain. No comparison to the pain I've experienced up to now. What have I done? My legs are lowered from the ceiling. Feeling begins to trickle up my legs. I'm plugged up again down there, lifted onto another bed, tucked in, and wheeled back to my room. By some random nurse I don't know and who can't wheel beds very well. Worse than Robin earlier in his agitated state.

She parks me in my big, lonely room and walks back out. If I need anything, I should buzz. I already know that. I've been here long enough to get that.

And now? After nearly bleeding to death, lying around in bed is boring. There's something I need to take care of. Get rid of the hemorrhoid pillow. I lift the covers and it's no longer there. Where is it? Who has it? Oh man, Helen, are you out of it. Must be the medication. Of course they made up the bed with fresh linens after the explosion of blood. So where has the pillow gotten to now? I can't ask, and don't want to. Maybe some stupid nurse just threw it out without even thinking. That would be the best. If somebody else had already taken care of the pillow.

I probably won't feel any pain for a while. So I might as well do something now. But what? I'm sure I'm not allowed to walk around. I'd rather not anyway—don't want everything to get ripped open again.

A knock.

Robin?

No, it's the candy striper. Something to keep me busy. This time I won't be as snippy as last time.

"Good day," she says.

I greet her back. Good start. I would love to keep her here for as long as possible, to stave off the boredom.

She can solve the telephone riddle.

"Do you guys pay to have the phone switched on for newly arrived patients?"

"Yes, we did that for you. You were so out of sorts from the pain that we figured we'd take care of that. We pay out of our funds. The patients repay us."

Too bad. I thought Robin had done it.

"Earlier this year I was here to be sterilized. Nobody did that for me then."

Come on, Helen, this information is of no concern to her.

"It's a new service we're providing."

I ask her for a favor. I would like a coffee from the cafeteria. And as long as she's down there, she could bring me some fresh grapes and a packet of trail mix. She can take

the money for it out of the drawer in the metal nightstand.
Along with whatever was advanced for the phone.

She agrees and leaves with the money.

While she's gone, I fill my glass with mineral water
from a bottle I took from the hospital supply. Bottoms up
into my mouth and then I spit it back into the bottle. I hold
my thumb over the top and shake it around. I repeat this
process three times.

I wait for her to return. I notice how tired I am. Close
my eyes. Despite the pills and the fact that the anesthesia
is probably still working a bit, I can feel the pain. It feels
as if they are still sewing up skin in my colon with metal
needles. They pull the thread tight and cut the end with
their teeth. Just the way mom always does it when she's
sewing. She does a lot of things with her mouth. Dangerous things, too. I remember as a kid watching her hang pictures with tacks. She would always put all the tacks in her
mouth and balance herself on a chair, taking one tack after
the other out of her mouth as she needed them. I close my
eyes with pain. Hold them closed for a long time.

I'm awoken by a knock as the candy striper returns.
That was fast. Of course she was faster than I was—she's
not an ass patient. It seemed like a long way to me.

I thank her for bringing me the things. And then I ask
her whether she would mind my asking her a few questions.
It's tough for me to maintain a normal conversation. Some-

thing's really brewing down inside me. The more painful it gets the more normal I try to come across. She says go ahead. I offer her some mineral water and she gratefully accepts. She goes to the nurses' station to get a clean glass. Stripers are allowed in there. And yet they can't give you a shot.

She comes back with a glass. She fills it to the brim and gulps it down. It makes me happy. It's as if we've already kissed. Without her even knowing, of course. Against her will even. As if she had been unconscious and I kissed her. That's how I'd describe our relationship. Kissing to dull the pain. It doesn't do much.

I feel close to her and smile at her. Suddenly I notice how nicely she's made-up. She's drawn a thin, light-blue line along the very edge of her bottom eyelids. It takes years of practice to be able to do that so well. She must have been making herself up for years. Probably started doing it back in school. Very good.

I ask her everything I can think of about her duties as a candy striper. How do you become one? Where do you apply? Are there many applicants? Are you allowed to pick which department you'll work in?

I think I must be talking funny. I wrench the questions out of myself. I'm almost too weak to talk. But with this feeling down there, I don't want to be alone. Now I know the most important aspects of the field of duty I'll join as soon as I am released.

I thank her sincerely. She understands and leaves.

"Thanks for your generous offer of water." She titters. She thinks it's funny because she has emphasized the word "generous" for comedic value, since it's just the hospital's own mineral water. I find it funny, too. But for other reasons.

As soon as she's gone, I'm filled with nasty thoughts. Where are my parents? For fucks sake! This is not happening. They've abandoned me here. I figured after Robin's call they'd be worried and come straight here. Nothing. Nobody here. A gaping abyss. I think much more about them than they do about me. Maybe I should stop thinking about them so much. They don't want me to take care of them. And I should finally give up on expecting anything from them. It doesn't get any clearer than this. I'm lying here having gone through an emergency operation and nobody turns up. That's the way it goes in our family. I know that if one of them had something like what I have, I wouldn't leave their side. That's the big difference. I'm more their parents than they are mine. I've got to stop that. Give it up, Helen. You're an adult now. You have to make your own way. Wake up to the fact that you're not going to change them. I can only change myself. Exactly. I want to live without them. Change of plan. It's just, in what way am I going to change my plan? What next? I need something to do. So I can think more clearly. When your hands are working, you brain works better, too.

Not to mention that I get sad when I have nothing to do.

I take the grapes and lay them in my lap on top of the sheet. Then I lean over to the metal nightstand and grab the bag of trail mix. I rip it open with my teeth. With my long thumbnail I slit open a grape along one side. Just the way you would a bread roll with a knife. I root around in the bag for a cashew nut, pull it out, and separate its two halves. It's easier than I thought it would be. As if they were already partially separated. I find a raisin in the bag and put it between the cashew halves. This stuffed cashew I push into the cut-open grape until it's in the middle. Now I just have to squeeze the grape back together so you can hardly see the cut. As if nothing's been done to it. Stuffed without a trace. My little masterpiece is finished. The truffle of poor students. The idea came to me the second I saw the candy striper. I knew I had to give her something to do for me— that's why they're here. These candy non-nurses in their odd-colored uniforms. And I wanted whatever she did for me to give me something to do later. It worked perfectly. I'm proud.

I'm going to transform all the grapes and trail mix into student truffles to give to my favorites. Lovely task you've found for yourself, Helen. The finished creations I place on the metal nightstand.

I love to stuff things into other things. What made me think of stuffing things when I looked at the candy striper I don't know. Sometimes I only realize after the fact, when someone has turned me on. Maybe that's what's going to happen in this case.

Back when we were still a cohesive family, mom would make stuffed birds on Christmas. She'd stuff a quail into a small chicken, the chicken into a duck, the duck into a small goose, and the goose into a turkey. The anus of each fowl would have to be widened with a few snips for the next one to fit through it. And then she'd roast the whole thing in the extra-large oven we had just so she could do this. A professional stove. A lot of gas comes out of those if you want it to. Between each set of birds mom would put strips of bacon because otherwise it would all dry out since it had to roast for so long for the heat to penetrate all the layers.

When it was done, we kids loved to watch it be sliced open.

The pain is practically knocking me out. I can't take it anymore. Helen, keep thinking about Christmas dinner. Keep your thoughts away from your butt. Back to your family. Think of something nice. Don't give in to the pain.

With the help of some big, sharp kitchen shears, the whole thing would be cut right down the middle so you'd get a perfect cross section of all the birds. It looked as if each one were pregnant with the next smaller one. The turkey was pregnant with the goose, the goose had a duck in its belly, the duck was pregnant with a chicken, and the chicken with a quail. It was hilarious. A parade of pregnant fetuses. And parsnips from the field next to our house roasted along with them. Delicious.

Once, a long time ago, I overheard my father late at night in the living room telling a friend of his that it was pretty awful for him to have to watch my birth. They had to give mom an episiotomy or else she would have torn from her pussy to her asshole. He said it had sounded as if they were cutting a stringy chicken down the middle with kitchen shears, through cartilage and other gristly parts. He imitated the sound several times that night. *Sniiip.* He was good at it. Each time the friend laughed loudly. You always laugh loudest at the things that scare you the most.

Just before I've used up all my student-truffle supplies, I go to put another finished work on the nightstand. With this motion, the stem with the last of the grapes attached to it falls to the floor.

I can't get out of bed now to pick it up. With the stitches in my ass, I don't want to move at all. With nothing more to do and my thoughts brought to a halt, I notice the pain getting worse and worse. I need a distraction and some stronger painkillers. I hit the buzzer. A nurse should be able to take care of it for me. While I'm waiting for help, I do nothing, for a change. I sit there and stare at the wall. Light light light green. What a subtle shade. I hate it when I can't take care of myself. It bugs me that I can't just hop down there and pick everything up. I don't like to depend on others. Doing things yourself is the best way. I trust myself the most. When it comes to applying sunscreen, for instance. But in all other matters in life, too.

She floats in. Pretty quick. Must not be too much buzzer action in the unit at the moment.

"Can you do me a favor and hand me those grapes?"

She crawls under the bed and collects them.

Instead of giving them back to me she takes them over to the sink. What does she think she's doing?

"I'll just rinse them off. They were on the floor, after all."

These hygiene fanatics would never think to ask: Do you want me to wash your grapes for you since they were on the disgustingly filthy hospital floor that's mopped twice a day? They just do it because they think everyone is as afraid of bacteria as they are. But that's not the case. In fact, in my case, it's just the opposite.

She rinses the grapes for quite some time in running water.

As she's rinsing them she says that she has the feeling they haven't been washed anyway, that they might still have toxic pesticides on them. They're still covered with that fuzzy, white film. A sure sign of having not been washed. Oh, please!

I don't say anything. I'm screaming inside, though. This idiotic notion of washing pesticides off fruit and vegetables is the biggest joke there is. My dad taught me. These days you learn it in school, too. In chemistry. The chemicals that are sprayed on produce to keep away vermin and fungus are so strong that they penetrate the skin of tomatoes and grapes. You can wash them until your fingers shrivel. Nothing comes off. If you don't want to eat pesticides with your fruit and vegetables, you shouldn't buy them at all. You're not going to cheat the poison industry with a few seconds of running water. I never wash fruit and vegetables. I don't think it removes any of the poisons.

The other reason the nurse feels the urgent need to wash my property is that people like her always think the floor is extremely filthy because people walk on it. In the imagination of these people, there must be a tiny particle of dog shit every few inches. That's the worst contaminant a hygiene fanatic can imagine. If kids pick things up from the ground and put them in their mouths they're always told: Be careful, there could be dog crap on that. Even though it's highly unlikely there's dog crap anywhere on it. And what if there is? What would be so bad about that? Dogs eat canned meat. The canned meat is turned into canned-meat-crap in their intestines and then lands on the street. Even if I ate spoonfuls from a pile of dog crap, I'm sure nothing would happen to me. So if a whiff of a trace of an unlikely particle of dog crap that somehow made its way into my hospital room sticks to a grape there beneath my bed and winds up in my mouth, nothing's going to happen.

She's finally finished with her nonsense.

I have my work materials back, washed against my will. I don't thank her.

"Could you please ask whether I can have some stronger pills or can take two at a time? What I've got isn't stopping the pain."

She nods and leaves.

I'm pissed off as I finish up my work. These stupid hygiene freaks drive me crazy. They are so unscientifically superstitious about bacteria. This pain is also driving me crazy. But I've hit upon my next good idea.

I know what I'm going to do now. I'm going to have a bowel movement. I can't stand up. I'll force myself. I need to make sure I can take care of myself. Which I normally don't have to worry about. Better to try to take my first bowel movement after emergency surgery here in a controlled environment near doctors than wherever I'll end up doing it if I'm discharged. I'm all out of sorts. I'm dizzy.

I'll make myself do it. It can't be that difficult. Maybe I'm still numb from the operation. It's possible that the pain will just keep getting worse from now on. In which case I'd rather try now. Now or never. Bite the bullet, Helen, and do it. And given what I've eaten in the last few days— granola as hard as wood chips—I should be ready to drop one. Off to the bathroom. First I need to get rid of the plug. What they manage to stuff up there is very long. I position myself in the reliable spread-legged stance above the bowl and think of the pain I felt when I ripped myself open. This is nothing by comparison. It works. I manage it. I do it well. In a death-defying feat, I push everything past the stitches and I'm home free. I don't need to tell anyone I was able to do this. But it's good for me to know. I'm one step closer to recovery. If I do end up abandoning my plan for my parents, this will have been a big waste of strength and suffering. We'll see. I rinse myself off and pat myself dry. Robin was right. It's a lot better than wiping with toilet paper. All the things he knows. We're a good match.

I go back over to the bed and stand next to it.

I have to do something. Have to. Doesn't matter what. The main thing is not to think about my parents or the pain in my asshole. My hands are shaking. I'm all tense. I wipe cold sweat from my brow. Cold sweat is creepy. The only other time you experience it is right before you faint. Little death. Aren't men's orgasms called that, too? Or is it something you say about animals? Which ones? I can't think straight. Not an enjoyable experience. This. Everything. I climb back into bed. I put all the trail-mix sculptures in my lap. I twist around so I can reach the back edge of the metal nightstand. I carefully lift up the bottle cap of tears and move it gingerly across the surface of the nightstand. I put it down on the edge closest to me, so I can easily reach it, and dunk the tip of my pointer finger in the salty water. I let a drop fall from my finger into the cut in each stuffed grape. I work carefully, as if my finger were an eyedropper. I have to conserve my tears so there's enough to go around. I already know to whom I'll offer them. I manage not to notice my pain for several minutes thanks to this tedious task. Once each grape has a drop in it, I put them all back in the trail mix bag.

As soon as I don't have anything to do, I panic. Think of something, Helen, anything. None of my friends, or I guess I should call them classmates, know I'm here. Only my parents know. And my brother. So the only visits I can hope for would be from my family.

And I might end up waiting a long time for that.

I didn't want to tell any of my classmates why I had to go to the hospital. I don't like the idea of them visiting me in the proctology unit. They all think I'm home with the flu. When I took off—how many days ago now?—because my ass hurt so bad, I told them I felt a flu coming on. That I was feeling achy. Nice word. Achy. And that I had to go home. I didn't have to worry about having my cover blown because none of them would stop by my house anyway. Nobody wants to hang out with a sick person. They like to go out, party, hang out in the park. They drink a lot and smoke pot, and you can't do that while visiting a sick person at home with their parents around. We only go around to people's places when their parents are on vacation. Otherwise, being outdoors is the best place for our hobbies. My parents are always pleased I get so much fresh air. But obviously, for me and my friends, hanging out isn't about getting fresh air in our lungs.

Robin comes into the room.

In his hand he's holding a plastic shot glass with two pills in it. These pills are shaped differently from any of the others. I guess the nurse said something about my pain. I don't even ask what they are. I hold out my hand, he plunks the two fat pills onto my palm, and I smack my hand to my mouth. Just like in the movies. The pills hit the back of my throat and I almost hurl. Quick, chase them with some hospital water. I cough. The uvula is a sensitive spot.

And unfortunately it's very closely tied to the gag reflex. Which can be very disruptive during sex. God didn't think that one out very well when he designed human beings. If I suck a cock during sex and want him to come in my mouth, I have to pay a hell of a lot of attention to make sure he doesn't shoot his sperm on my uvula. Because then I would puke immediately. Been through it all, our Helen. Obviously I want to take the cock as deep into my throat as I can—it really makes a striking visual impact. I look like a sword swallower. But I really have to watch out for my uvula. It's a pain. Everything has to tiptoe around it.

"Robin, did you call my parents before the emergency operation?"

"Oh, you know what, I forgot to tell you with all the commotion. I was only able to leave messages. Didn't reach them directly. Sorry. I'm sure they'll come at some point. Once they've listened to their messages."

"Sure."

He tidies the room. The table at the foot of the bed, something in the bathroom. He neatly organizes everything on the metal nightstand.

I stare straight ahead and say under my breath, "Any other parents whose daughter was in a situation like this would either stay with her in the hospital the whole time or sit by the phone at home so as not to miss any emergency calls. The trade-off, I guess, is that I have more freedom. Thanks."

I ask him if he wants to taste my new specialty. I've invented a new dish. It's that boring for me here, Robin.

I hold out the trail mix bag with the tear-grapes in it. If someone eats a woman's tears, the two of them are forever bound to each other.

I explain what he has in his hand. I leave out the part about the tears. He bravely sticks the modified grape in his mouth. First I hear the skin of the grape burst, then the crack of the nut. With his mouth full he says he likes it and asks if he can have some more. Of course. He eats one after the other. He continues to clean up and keeps coming back to the metal nightstand to pop another grape in his mouth.

The pills aren't working yet. I'm tense and tired. Pain is exhausting. It's very hard to create attachments with people in a hospital room. I have the feeling everybody wants to get out of my room quickly. Maybe it doesn't smell good in here. Or I don't look good. Or maybe people just want to distance themselves from sickness and pain. The nurses' station has a magical pull on all the nurses and care-givers, including Robin. I can hear them laughing out there in ways they never do in here. As a patient I'll soon be gone; as employees they'll still be here. That creates a barrier. But I'll break it down soon. Even with no medical training I'll join them as soon as I'm released. As a candy striper I'll be allowed in their break room and drink sparkling water with them. For the first time, I have the feeling that Robin is trying to stay near me. He doesn't leave. He keeps tidying. In places he's already just cleaned up. It makes me happy. I've managed to create an attachment.

I pick up the phone. I dial mom's number. Nobody answers. Answering machine.

"Hi, it's me. When is somebody going to come visit me? I'm in pain and I have to stay here longer than I thought. At least send my brother by. He hasn't been here yet. I would visit him if he had an operation down under."

I hang up. Slam it down. Of course, on an answering machine you can't tell the difference between a friendly hang up and an angry one.

I pick up the phone again and ask the dial tone: "And why did you try to kill yourself and Tony, mom? Are you sick? What's wrong?"

You coward, Helen.

I'm spent.

I'm talking to myself, and a little bit to Robin.

"I can't take it anymore. Not by myself. I have to constantly beg for painkillers. I lie to everyone about my bowel movements so I can stay here as long as possible in order to bring my parents together in this room. But they never come. And they'll never show up at the same time. How is my plan supposed to work? What a load of shit. A massive load of shit. I'm an idiot and want things nobody else wants."

I can feel the muscles in my shoulders tightening up. That always happens when I realize that everything's pointless and that I can't control things. My shoulders start to rise toward my ears because of the tension and I cross my arms and try to push them back down with my hands. I close my eyes and try to calm myself with exaggerated deep breathing. Doesn't work. Never works. My butt is burning, it's killing me, and my shoulders are attaching themselves to my ears.

My grandmother has been so tense for her whole life that she doesn't have any shoulders at all anymore. Her arms come right out of her ears. Right next to her head. Once, when I was still young and nice, I went to massage her and she immediately let out a bloodcurdling scream. Then she told me that the muscles there had been so tense for so many years that the lightest touch felt to her as if someone were poking around in an open wound. But that's not reason enough for her to try to do something about it. She just has all her blouses altered at the tailor so the arms are sewn right onto the collar—otherwise the extra flower-print fabric of the shoulders would hang there in big pouches. If I don't want to end up like that, I'm going to have to come up with a way to avoid it. But how? Gymnastics? Massages? Ditch my family?

As a result of getting my back slammed in the car door, my doctor used to have me get regular massages. The first thing I'd ask each new masseuse was whether they'd ever had a male client get a hard-on during a massage.

Every one of them said yes. I'd act as if I was sympathetic, that I was as disgusted as they were about the boners.

Ah, men. In reality I was hoping to hear a story that would turn me on. I mean, what do these people think?

How can a man avoid getting a hard-on when a woman is massaging all around his cock and balls, like on his upper thigh? I get wet from that, too. It's just that with women you can't see the excitement.

I'll start with that. I need to take the bull by the horns so I don't end up like grandma. When I get out of here, I'm scheduling some more massages.

Where is Robin? I can hear him puttering around in the bathroom. Is it possible he's worried about me? Though I have downed some strong medicine—maybe he's just obligated to keep an eye on me. That could be it.

When was the last time I ate something?

Who cares. I only want to eat painkillers. Nothing else. The pain in my ass keeps getting worse. My head is spinning.

Grandma can probably lie on her side very easily. The breadth of normal shoulders can get in the way when lying on your side. When she lies on her side, it's a straight line from her ear right down along her arm. Much more comfortable. Maybe I won't make any appointments for massages after all. I should have a closer look at grandma. Then I'll decide.

Robin comes over to the bedside.

"Is it bad?"

"Yes."

"In my experience, it'll start to get better by tonight at the latest. Tomorrow you'll probably be able to handle it without any medicine, and if you have a bowel movement with no bleeding, you'll probably be allowed to go home."

That's not possible. They'd send me home in this condition? That's it for my plan. Definitely. But I had already screwed it up. Pointless. This whole thing.

"Home? Nice."

Shit.

Robin, I don't want to go home. And I already had a bowel movement. I've fooled you all. Sorry. All because of my messed-up family. I have nowhere to go. I have to stay here. Forever.

I don't want Robin to leave.

Maybe I can distract myself from the pain with a bit of conversation until the medicine starts working.

"Robin, can I tell you a secret?"

"Oh, man. What is it, Helen?"

"It's not what you think." Of course. I need to dispel the reputation I have with him. "It's got nothing to do with my ass or nakedness or anything. I just wanted to show you my little family."

He looks annoyed, but nods.

I turn to the windowsill and lift up the Bible.

"What is all that?" he asks.

I put the Bible down next to me in bed.

I give him a long lecture about my hobby, growing avocado trees.

He listens closely. I manage to keep him in my room for a long time. For the moment I don't have to share him with other ass patients.

As I bring my presentation to a close, he takes off his white hospital clogs and climbs onto my bed. He looks at the avocado pits up close. This makes me very happy. Nobody's ever shown so much interest in this hobby of mine.

He says he wants to try it out himself at home. Says they look pretty.

"If you want, you can pick one out and take it home with you."

"No, I couldn't do that. You've already put so much work into them."

"Yes, and for exactly that reason, you should take one."

He hesitates. He must be trying to figure out whether or not it's allowed. Strong sense of duty it seems to me. Always following the rules, this Robin.

"Well, okay. If you're absolutely sure you want to give one away. I'll take this one here."

He points to the nicest one of all. A light-yellow pit with touches of light pink. And a healthy, dark green sprout. Good choice.

"It's yours."

He picks up the glass and carefully lifts it across the bed, keeping it balanced so the water doesn't spill. He slips back into his shoes and stands in front of my bed with the avocado pit. He seems really happy. We smile at each other.

He walks out.

I wrap my arms around my rib cage. It occurs to me that I'll be released soon. My body and I shrug inwardly, and with that comes a gush of something down below. Warm. It could be anything. Out of any opening. I can't distinguish anything down there at the moment.

I feel around with a finger. My first thought is that it's a fluid leaking out pussywise. I make my finger magically reappear from under the sheet and see that the fluid is red. Got it.

I forgot to put in a tampon. With all the unusual bleeding I completely forgot about the routine bleeding. The bed is covered. I'm covered. Smeared with blood.

Okay. This is my own problem. I'm not going to ring for Robin and ask him to run and bring me something again. I don't want him to think I've fallen in love with him and I'm just sitting here thinking up reasons to ring. I am in pain and really did need the pills. It's fine to ring for that. But this would be too much. I don't want to get on his nerves.

Though it's also all right if he thinks I've fallen in love with him. Because I have. So there's no reason he can't be the first to know. But I can handle menstrual blood by myself. I've always managed to in the past—except that one time at my aunt's.

I grab the plastic container from the windowsill and pull out two squares of gauze and a piece of paper towel. I also take the opportunity to pull out my old tampon. Time for it to go. I'm sure it's already spread enough bacteria. Into the trash it goes before anyone has noticed it.

I can see condensation in the plastic container. It's warm on the windowsill. On the inside of the box, droplets of moisture have formed. When they get too big and can't hold on to the sides of the container anymore, they drip down, pulling other droplets with them. The droplets running down the sides seek the easiest path and leave a tiny, zigzagging trail of destruction behind, the same way a river does on a bigger scale. Then the droplets can join to form a fetid, fermenting puddle and bubble up into new steam droplets to cling to the sides of the container. Whoever stays up longest . . .

I need to examine my gown. If there's blood on it, I'll flip out. There's no way I'm asking for another one.

Lucky. All clean. I hadn't pushed it under myself properly. Good. I shift to the side to have a look at the mess. Not as much has come out as I thought. Good.

I lay one piece of the padding down with the plastic side up and the other on top of it with the plastic side down.

I can do it with my eyes closed now. Nice to have something to do again.

I rip the paper towel in half and with one half wipe all around the folds of my pussy, soaking up as much blood as possible.

The other half I fold lengthwise so I have a long, thin, flat piece of toweling. I roll this up into a short, thick sausage and shove it as far into my pussy as I can. Take that, American tampon industry!

Then I sit on the soft gauze pads.

Ta-dah!

Done.

How well you take care of yourself, Helen.

I'm proud of myself. That doesn't happen very often, and it makes me smile warmly inside.

If I'm in such a good mood and thinking such nice thoughts, that must mean the pain medication has kicked in.

I concentrate on trying to feel my wounded ass and realize nothing hurts. I just veer back and forth from pain to no pain in here.

I want to get up and walk around.

I've perfected my method of slowly getting out of bed so well that it would be a shame if I were pronounced healed and released.

I lie on my stomach and scoot my body, feet first, sideways toward the edge of the bed until I'm in the shape of a right angle with just my upper body on the bed and my feet on the ground. I call this gymnastics position "Helen kicks herself out of bed."

The best view of it is from the doorway. Open tree-top angel gown, naked, wounded ass spread open to the door. I snap my upper body up and stand.

I stretch my right arm high in the air the way we were taught to after a tumbling routine. Smile wide and stretch your body so far out in the direction of your hand that your heels briefly leave the mat. I snap my right hand down to the side of my thigh. Nod my head, curtsy, and wait for applause. Silence. Wipe the smile off my face. What can you do, Helen, you always give your best performances when nobody's watching. It's just the way you are.

I'm not in any pain and want to move my body. Where should I go? Not outside. Don't feel like running into other people. And besides, I'd either have to put on an ass parade in the hallway or put on underwear.

Do I even have any underwear here? I can't remember what mom brought me.

There's the first thing I can do on my tour of the room. Have a look. I go to the wardrobe. Open the door. It's true. Pajama pants and T-shirts. Untouched. I've used hospital gowns right from the start. Haven't put on any of my own things.

Robin said I might be released as soon as tomorrow.

Time to pack my bag if it's going to go according to that plan.

I'm not going to be able to make it work with my parents. It was a good plan. But they haven't even shown up despite the emergency operation. I would love to continue trying to make my plan work. But it's not going to happen here. They don't visit often enough, and I'd have to have something much worse to be able to stay any longer. They won't let me stay here long enough to pull it off. It's nice here. Nicer than at home, at least.

Maybe I can go somewhere else beside home if I'm going to get kicked out of here so soon?

I pick up the empty bag on the bottom of the wardrobe and ball it up as small as I can. I stick it into the chrome trash can on the metal nightstand. Now my things will just have to stay in the wardrobe—they don't have a bag to travel in.

Come on, Helen, that's absolutely ridiculous. You can think of somewhere to go.

I have an idea. I take the bag back out of the trash can.

Move around some more. As long as I can't feel my ass, it's almost as if I'm here on vacation. On drugs.

From the nightstand I move along the edge of the bed to the corner that sticks out into the room. Then around the short side of the bed to the windowsill.

And back. Once. Faster. Twice. With ever-faster steps I go back and forth five times until I'm winded.

All this walking strains my legs. My muscles have already atrophied in the few days I've been lying around.

Still standing, I hike up the gown so I can look at my legs. I stretch one leg out onto the bed, then I take it back down and stretch out the other one to have a look. They're thinner. They look funny. A bit like granny legs—hardly any muscle, white skin, and long hair. Ugh.

I hadn't thought about that at all during the entire time here in the hospital. When you're in pain, you don't necessarily feel like shaving.

Now, though.

I throw myself onto the bed. Too hard. Despite the pills I feel pain rise from my ass up through my back. Take it easy, Helen, don't flip out.

It's nice not to have any pain and you want to keep it that way for a while. So watch it with the jerky movements.

I grab the phone and dial mom's number. Answering machine again. Have they all gone on vacation in my absence? When was the last time I saw one of them?

It's been days.

It's difficult to figure out exactly how long it's been. Or how long I've been here. Probably has something to do with the painkillers and the pain and with my general drug consumption. These gaps in my memory.

"It's me again. Did you get my other message? If either of you is still even thinking of visiting me, do it fast. Tony, you haven't come to see me at all. If you do come, can you bring one of mom's dresses and a pair of her shoes? Thanks. See you soon. It's already evening."

Oh, man. It sucks when you have to depend on blood relatives. Now I have to wait until somebody brings me those things.

I get out of bed in slow motion and walk to the door. I open it a crack and peek out. There was some kind of noise coming from out there. Something's going on.

Dinner service. They're pushing around multilevel towers stacked with trays and stopping in front of each door. Maybe I'll get some normal food tonight. Not the usual granola and whole-grain bread. If I were to tell them I've long since had a bowel movement, I'd get something better to eat. But I'm not saying anything.

I slowly go back to bed and get in to wait for feeding time.

There's a knock at the door.

I offer a very friendly "Good evening." It's some female nurse. I can't tell them apart. All of them unfuckable.

"Good evening. In a good mood, are we, Miss Memel? How are you—had a bowel movement yet?"

"Not yet, but thanks for asking. What's on the menu tonight?"

"Unfortunately just whole-grain bread for you. You know that's the situation until your first bowel movement."

"I'd rather have granola."

I already have everything I need for that right here.

"What are the other patients having tonight?"

"The meat dish is a roast with peas, potatoes, and gravy. The vegetable dish is a cabbage stew."

That sounds like paradise to me. For one thing because it's warm. I only get cold food, and after awhile it leaves you cold inside, too. I'm on the verge of telling this nanny that I shat ages ago.

But then, although I'd get one warm meal, I'd just be sent home. That's too high a price to pay.

I need some more time to figure out where I'm going when I leave.

"Thanks. I can mix it up myself."

With slouched shoulders, I shovel three spoonfuls of granola into the bowl then pull the trail mix bag out of the drawer and put three grape creations on top. Tonight Helen's having granola with tears.

When I can't feel the pain, life is fun. I pop the aluminum cherry of the little milk container by sticking a hole in it with the plastic tube stuck to the side of the box. I turn the box upside down and squeeze the milk into the bowl until the box is empty. Dad used to lecture us about not using the word "straw" because the things weren't made of straw anymore. But I can't believe they were ever made out of straw. How could you pop the cherry on a drink box with a piece of straw? It would buckle immediately. Surely they were always made out of plastic and are called straws just because somebody thought they looked like stalks of straw.

I eat my cold dinner fast.

There's a soft knock on the door as I'm downing the last bite.

That's not a nurse. They always knock louder and more confidently. And nobody walks in. Definitely not a nurse. I'm betting it's my father. He also has a weak handshake. Everyone complains about it. Guess he doesn't have muscular hands. Not strong enough to knock solidly on doors, either.

"Come in."

The door opens slowly. Man, oh, man, so gingerly compared to the nurses.

It's my brother's head. Must be genetic. Inherited weak hand muscles from our father.

"Tony."

"Helen?"

"Come on in. You just missed dinner. Thanks for visiting me."

He has a bag in his hand.

"Did you bring the things I wanted?"

"Of course. But what are they for?"

"It's a secret."

He looks at me. I look at him. Is that all the conversation we're going to manage?

Okay, damn the torpedoes.

"Tony, you don't like hospitals, do you? That's why you haven't visited me up to now."

"Yeah, but you know that. I'm sorry, Helen."

"Do you want me to tell you why you don't like it here?"

He chuckles. "As long as it's not bad."

"It is."

His smile disappears. He looks at me anxiously.

Go ahead, Helen, out with it.

"When you were really small, mom tried to kill herself. She wanted to take you with her. She put sleeping pills down your throat and took a bunch herself. When nice little Helen came home, you two were lying unconscious on the kitchen floor and gas was streaming out of the oven. Against mom's will, I saved you guys before the house blew up or you suffocated to death. At the hospital they pumped your stomachs and you guys had to stay here a long time."

He looks at me sadly. I think he already suspected it. His eyelids take on a light-blue hue. Handsome boy. But the muscles around his eyes are weak, too.

He's silent for a long time. Doesn't move an inch.

Then he stands up and slowly makes his way to the door. He opens it and, as he's walking out, he says, "That's why I always have those fucked-up dreams. She's going to get hers."

My family is even farther up shit's creek than it already was.

Is that my fault?

Just because I told Tony the truth?

You can't be silent forever. Lies. For the sake of keeping the peace in the family? Peace through lies. We'll see what happens. With a lot of things I do, I only think about the consequences after I've already done them.

The plan to get my parents back together is now completely out the window.

This is driving me slowly crazy. I'm confined here and everyone else just comes and goes as they please. And I'm sure they're all doing things out there I don't know about. I'd love to be doing things with them, I think for a second. But that's bullshit. Out there our family's even more torn apart, each of us only out for ourselves. At least with my ass bound to this bed my relatives' paths cross mine every once in a while.

There's a knock and someone rushes in. I think for a second my brother has come back to talk more about his near-death at the hands of my mother.

But the person standing there is wearing big, white hospital clogs and white linen pants.

A doctor.

I look up. Dr. Notz.

He better not release me. I'll chain myself to the bed.

"Good evening, Miss Memel. How are you feeling?"

"If you want to know whether I've had a bowel movement, just ask, please. There's no point in beating around the bush."

"Before I discuss your bowel movements, I want to know how you're doing with the pain."

"Fine. The nurse gave me some pills a few hours ago. Supposedly the last ones, if I understood correctly."

"Exactly. You'll have to get used to dealing with it without pills. And all this pressure to have a bowel movement doesn't seem to be working, either. With some patients we have to abandon our usual requirement of their having a bowel movement with no bleeding here at the hospital. The pressure is too much for them and they get too tense."

What? He's just going to release me right now and have me crap at home?

"For that reason I'd like to suggest you go home and see how it goes in peace and quiet. And if it starts to bleed again, just come back. Our opinion is there's no point to keeping you here."

Our opinion? I only see one person. Whatever. Crap. What now? What am I going to do? My wonderful plan irrevocably ruined by Notz.

"Yeah, sounds sensible. Thanks."

"You don't seem to be as pleased as most patients are when they're released. I like to deliver the happy news personally."

I'm sorry to spoil your fun, Notz. But I don't want to go home.

"I'm happy, I'm just not showing it."

And now get out of here, you. I need to think.

"I won't say 'see you later' because I would only see you later if something went wrong at home with the healing process. So, hopefully, see you never."

Yeah, I get it. Ha ha. I'm not a moron. See you never.

"I'll say 'see you later.' Once I'm better I'm going to become a candy striper. They already know. Do something meaningful with my life. I've already applied. I'm sure we'll run into each other in the hall at some point."

"Lovely. Good. See you later."

Out. Door closed.

Think!

My last chance. To leave my family. I'll call my father and tell him I've been released. He should pick me up tonight. I dial his number. He answers. He doesn't apologize for not being there after the emergency operation. As expected. I tell him everything, tell him I've been released, tell him he should come get me.

Come on, Helen, what's the point. Just ask.

"Dad, what do you do?"

"Are you serious? You don't know?"

"Not exactly."

Actually not at all.

"I'm an engineer."

"Aha. And would you like it if I became an engineer?"

"Yes, but you're no good at math."

Dad often hurts my feelings. He never notices, though.

Engineer. I write it out in my head and read it back to myself.

I do the same with my mom. No asking her what she does. I already know that: she's a hypocrite. I leave another message, telling her I'm being released tonight and that she needs to pick me up, preferably with Tony. It's possible she never wants to see me again after what I told Tony. We'll see.

Now, Helen, you have to do what you planned.

I get out of bed. Finally. I won't be getting back in it. I pick up the bag that I'd previously hidden in the trash can.

I stuff all the clothes from the wardrobe into it. I throw in all the stuff from the bathroom. The bag smells a bit like old menstrual blood. But I'm the only one who would notice that.

I put the bag aside and lean over the bed. I snatch the Bible and rip out a few pages.

I go back and forth to the sink to empty the avocado glasses. I dump out all the water.

I stack the glasses inside each other, put them in the bag and wrap the leg of my pajama pants around them.

I leave the toothpicks in my babies and wrap each one in a page of the Bible. Wrapped up, I put them all in the bag.

Now to clean out the nightstand drawer. I'll leave the crucifix here. I look around the room. I sit on the edge of the bed and let my legs dangle like I did as a child.

There's no sign of me left in the room. It's as if I was never here. All that remains are some invisible bacterial clues here and there. Nothing visible.

I ring the buzzer. Hopefully he's still around.

It occurs to me that they may have actually been worried about me. That they may have thought I was holding it in out of fear of the pain. I'm sure that happens all the time in this unit. But for such an extended period of time?

I'd like to have seen whether they would try more aggressive measures at some point. Like an enema. It wouldn't have been a problem for me. Let them come at me with their tubes and liquids. They couldn't wear me down with that.

It takes a while for someone to come. Though I'm hoping it's Robin who comes, not just someone.

I hoist my legs up onto the bed and turn myself around. I want to look out the window. Can't see anything. There's nothing out there. Just me and my room reflected in the glass. I stare at myself for a long time and notice how tired I look. Amazing how pain and painkillers break you down. They could go ahead and add some happy-happy uppers to the mix.

I don't look good. Not that I ever do. But I really look bad now. My hair's greasy and sticking up all over the place. It's the way I imagine I'll look when I have my first nervous breakdown. All the women in my family have nervous breakdowns. Not that they have so much to do. Maybe that's the problem. I'm sure it'll strike me like a bolt of lightning one day. Just sitting there doing nothing one minute, crazy the next.

Maybe before all hell breaks loose here I can wash my hair.

There's a knock at the door. Please, please, nonexistent God, let it be Robin.

The door opens. Some woman is standing there. At least she's dressed the same way as Robin.

"Has Robin already left?"

"His shift is over, yes, but he hasn't left."

"Could you do me a huge favor and ask him to stop by for a second before he takes off?"

"Sure."

"Great, thanks."

Thank you, thank you, thank you. Run. Fast. Little nurse.

There's something brewing with the Memels.

If Robin's gone, that's it for my plan.

What's this about washing your hair, Helen? Normally you don't care how you look in a situation like this, right? Robin thought you were cute when you had a blister hanging out of a lesion in your ass. And that's gone. Clearly an aesthetic improvement.

The greasy hair can function like my stuff-your-face position, to test whether he really likes me.

The hair stays dirty. I comb it down a little with my fingers.

The door opens. Robin.

"What's up? I'm just about to head home. You're lucky —you barely caught me."

You, too. Because if you want to, you can take me home with you.

"You've packed up your things? Have you been released?"

He looks sad. He thinks he has to say good-bye now. I nod.

He's covered his white uniform with a light-and-dark-blue checkered raincoat. Looks good. A timeless classic.

No time to lose.

"Robin, I've lied to all of you. I've already had a bowel movement. By that measure I'm healthy. You know—no bleeding. Well, in the front. But not in the back. You understand what I mean. I just wanted to stay in the hospital as long as possible because I thought I could bring my family together here. We're not even a family anymore, actually, but I was hoping to get my parents together again in this room. But that's crazy. They don't want that. They have new partners whom I ignore so much I don't even know their names. I don't want to go home to my mom. Dad's left. My mom's so unhappy she tried to kill my little brother. I'm eighteen. I can decide for myself where I want to go. Can I come live with you?"

He laughs.

Out of embarrassment? At me? I look at him appalled.

He comes up to me. He stands in front of me and wraps his arms around me. I start to cry. I cry more and more. I sob. He strokes my greasy hair. He's passed the test.

I smile briefly midsob.

"I guess you have to figure out whether it's allowed."

His jacket is tear-repellent.

"Yes."

"Yes you have to find out whether it's allowed, or yes I can come home with you?"

"Come with me."

He picks up my bag and helps me out of bed.

"Can you take my bag to the car and pick me up? I have to clear something up with my family."

"I'd love to. But I don't have a car. Just a bike."

Me on the back with my fucked-up ass. That's the last thing I need. But that's what we'll do.

"Is your place far? I could make it a little ways on a rear rack."

"It's not far. Really. I'll take your bag to the nurses' station and wait for you to ring the buzzer. Then I'll pick you up. I have your bag so there's no turning back."

"You won't have to wait long. Can I get one thing out of the bag?"

I root around inside and find my pen. I need that. And a T-shirt and a pair of socks.

He caresses my face, kisses me, and nods at me a few times. I guess it's supposed to give me courage to deal with my family.

"No turning back," I say to him as he leaves.

The door closes.

I pull my mom's dress and shoes out of the bag Tony brought me.

I stuff the bag into the wardrobe. Don't need it anymore. It would only ruin the picture.

I lay the dress out on the floor with the neck opening facing the wall. I place the shoes below the bottom of the dress at roughly the proper distance.

The T-shirt I fold up so it looks like a piece of children's clothing. I roll the socks a little so they look like kids' socks. I lay these things next to the adult female "body." From the Tupperware container I pull out two square gauze pads and fold them up. I lay them where the figures' heads would be. Their pillows.

The larger figure gets long hair. I pull out one strand after the other from my head and lay them one at a time on the pillow. You can't see them. I keep stepping back to see whether they're noticeable if you're just standing in the room and don't know what you're looking at. At some point I stop pulling them out one at a time. Taking too long. I yank hair out of my scalp in bunches and lay it on the pillow until I think you can make it out well enough. It doesn't hurt as much as I thought it would. Probably because of the painkillers. And now the child's hair. It needs to be short. I can rip every strand I pluck out into three pieces of hair for the child. I lay enough short hair on the child's pillow so it's clearly visible.

Now it's obvious that a woman and a boy are lying there.

With the pen I draw an oven and burners on the wall at the heads of the bodies. With a bit of perspective, as if the stove's receding into the wall.

At the top of the oven door I cut into the wallpaper with the pen. I use my fingernails to claw along the oven door and then pull at the wallpaper, ripping it down from the top to the floor. Now it looks like a real, open oven door.

I step back and take a good look at what my relatives are about to discover.

My good-bye letter. The reason I'm leaving. Silence.

There they are. My mother and my brother. Just the way I found them. They all hoped I'd forget. You can't forget something like that. And through their silence it loomed ever larger for me. Never faded.

I ring the buzzer one last time and wait for my Robin.

The entire time I'm waiting I stare at mom and Tony. I can smell gas.

Robin comes in.

"Get me out of here."

We leave.

I close the door behind me. I press a big puff of air out of my lungs, exhaling loudly.

We walk slowly down the hall.

We don't hold hands.

Suddenly he stops and puts the bag down. He's changed his mind.

No. He steps behind me and ties the gown closed over my bum. He wants to cover me up in public. Good sign. He picks up the bag again and we walk on.

"If I'm living with you, I guess you'll want to sleep with me?"

"Yeah, but I won't do you up the ass for now."

He laughs. I laugh.

"I'll only sleep with you if you can suck a pony's insides out through its asshole."

"Is that even possible—or do you not want to sleep with me?"

"I just always wanted to say that to a guy. Now I have. And I do want to. But not today. I'm too tired."

We walk to the glass door.

I smack the button, the door swings open, I throw back my head and scream.

The Dirty Girl

Controversial *Wetlands* author, Charlotte Roche, talks
about bodily functions, shaving pubic hair,
and why there are so few euphemisms
for female masturbation.

BY NINA POWER

Charlotte Roche is a curious mix of old radicalism and new daring. A well-known music and talk show host in Germany, Roche has produced a minor literary scandal, not to mention a major commercial success, with her first novel, *Wetlands*. The first German book to make Amazon's worldwide best-seller list, *Wetlands* is a savage, darkly humorous attempt to depict the contours of female anatomy and desire that has appalled as many as it has delighted with its graphic details.

Set in a hospital, it follows the thoughts and strange encounters of eighteen-year-old Helen Memel, the victim of an unfortunate attempt at intimate shaving. It is hard not to see Roche's rebellion against the unwritten demand that women be shaven, constantly presentable, and perpetually desirable as, in part, an attack on the television culture that made her name. Helen is everything a female TV host cannot be: ill, self-involved, and obsessed with obscenity. But *Wetlands* is more than just a complaint against the sexual double standards of contemporary life. It points to an odd paradox: for all the hedonism of an apparently liberated culture in which women can drink and screw with the best of them (think *Sex and the City*), the language we use to describe this behavior and these unleashed desires is profoundly outdated or, more often, simply absent. For all the inventively silly and explicit ways to describe male masturbation, for example, it is hard to think of many euphemisms for the female equivalent. Choking the oyster, anyone?

Roche creates a world—a "Wetlands" indeed—in which there are new words to describe the weirdness of the female body and the ambivalence of sexual encounters. It's a damp and claustrophobic universe, but one that reminds us of how far we have to go to overcome deepseated embarrassments about basic biological facts. Roche is a strange poster girl for such a progressive operation, elfin and brazen in equal parts, but in person she neatly captures the contradictions of a contemporary femininity that can't decide whether it wants to be low-down and dirty or prim and proper (or both at the same time).

In Helen, Roche has created a character that promises a certain kind of liberation—the right to be sick and sexy, the right to be damaged and confident, the right to speak about anything and everything without shame. To combine such earnestness with comedy is a tough feat, but Roche pulls it off with a rare charm: television's loss is literature's gain. I caught up with Roche at her British publisher's office in London, where she talked about female fantasies and the fun of creating an alter ego.

In Germany the book was primarily bought by women. But perhaps there wasn't as much discussion, or the kind of discussion, about it that you wanted?

On the one hand, the reception was extremely negative. They made a big scandal out of it. They said, "We don't want this, this is disgusting, this is not literature." On the other hand, there were very intellectual women writing very nice things about it. It's something to do with the sexes: Men have a laugh, or they think it's disgusting. Women think, "Ah, this has something to do with me," and they get into it.

It has sometimes been read in the context of chick lit—lightweight, a bit romantic, Sex and the City-type novels with pink covers . . .

The pink corner in the bookshop!

. . . and your book has been seen as a subversion of this genre, like you're trying to undo "women's literature" by pushing it to an extreme, or that you're trying to do something pornographic. Is the book pornographic, or simply explicit?

I think "pornographic" is the wrong word. We use "pornographic" because we don't have enough words to describe what it is. I wanted to write something original, [to] be honest, and the way I write things is explicit because that's the way I see things. I am not a person who would say, "Oh, this is disgusting" and look away. I would look at the disgusting thing and describe it in a very detailed way. Maybe even to overcome the disgusting. You look at it as long as you can and then it's not disgusting anymore.

You have said that at the very moment where the reader might get aroused, you deflate the desire. There's a sense in which it could excite you, but then you go further, do something else.

I wrote it so that it would be a bit horny at some points, because I wanted it to be a realistic, honest book about the body. But it also has to have all the taboos that we think are disgusting; human, liquid, disgusting stuff. So I always imagine a man reading it and having an erection [raises finger] and then reading and wanting to wank and then [lowers finger] . . .

I wanted to write things that I have problems with, things that I am embarrassed about, like writing your heart out. The big misunderstanding is that I am so cool, so open, because I've written this book. It's not at all the case. There are things in the book that are my lifetime problems, like going to the toilet in public lavatories. As soon as someone would walk in, I would stop because I feel so embarrassed. It's all about being a woman and not being allowed to shit.

I think a lot of the book is about recognizing these feelings of embarrassment. Contemporary women are supposed to be liberated, hedonistic, you can go out and get drunk, sleep around. But if we don't have the words to describe the range of experiences other than the old negative ones, then nothing has really changed.

If we don't have the words and we don't talk about it, then I would also suggest that we don't even think about it. I have this theory. If you tell any man, "Today I am your sexual servant. You can tell me whatever you want and I'll do it to you," every man would think of twelve things to do. Men have fantasies; they have words for everything. They could tell a woman, "Lie down, do this, lick this." But if a man said to me, "I am your sexual servant, what do you want me to do?" I would be blank. There's nothing even in my head to allow myself to think what I actually like.

I seem to be a modern, self-confident woman, and people would think that kind of woman would be into dirty talk, high heels, drugs, fucking around. But as soon as it comes to the secret intimacy of my own fantasies, there's almost nothing there. So for me it was about sitting down and thinking, what does the vagina look like? What do all the little bits look like? What could you call them? It was therapy for myself to actually think about this, which I wasn't doing before.

The contemporary woman is supposed to be sexually available, as you say, but when a woman is sick, she ceases to exist as a sexual being. Which is why the illness theme in Wetlands *is really interesting.*

Very often, lately, people have come up to me and say "You look tired," and I hate it. Women are supposed to always look fit and healthy and pretty. But everything that is sick and tired is all very human—and I think that being human is a big taboo. When people say that the book is about taboos, I ask them, what do you mean? Shit? Piss? Menstruation?

Menstruation is in many ways extremely annoying and quite disturbing, for all its normalcy. But it isn't really spoken about that much, is it?

The problem with taboos is that you think you're the only one. And Helen always wants to know: Does it smell the same with other women? How do other women's vaginas look? We're all completely isolated. It's not a group of women that menstruate; we're on our own. But where does that come from? Mothers still don't think it's a good thing to be a woman.

The mother in Wetlands *says that you can't ever be clean enough.*

You can clean and clean, and you won't ever stop being dirty. My mother tried to raise me in a very liberated way. I was allowed to have sex at a very early age. I was allowed to bring boys over to the house because she didn't want me fucking around in the woods. She's a very strong, political feminist, and she raised me in a very feminist way, teaching me that as a girl, I can do everything a boy can do, there's no problem. But still, the sexual stuff . . . she never managed to teach me that masturbation is a good thing. Although my mother was liberated, I still feel that if I have dirty knickers [underpants], I have to hide them from my husband.

Mothers tend to be almost proud of their son's sexual conquests, whereas girls have to keep quiet about it.

Exactly. I have so many arguments with people who say, "Look at *Sex and the City*. Women can do everything. We can fuck around." But look at families with young teenagers: They start making jokes about the boy age twelve or thirteen; they leave tissues by his bed. But what mother can manage to teach her daughter that it's a good thing to menstruate— or nothing terrible, at least? That it's a good thing to have sex, to have breasts? I know stories from women of my age, and the mothers would say, "Can you please hide your period from your brothers, because I don't want to have to explain what it is."

In the book, Helen pays for sex with other women. Why doesn't she have sexual relationships with women without the involvement of money?

I thought it was a nice idea, because she doesn't know who to ask. It's like going to a psychiatrist because you can't talk to anybody else about your problems.

In the literature of the Enlightenment, the prostitute sleeps with politicians, the clergy, so she's cynical and clever. She understands power. She's also a materialist, because she understands how bodies work. Helen reminds me of this type of literary heroine.

The good thing about prostitutes is that you can get to the point straight-away. They're not shocked about anything you ask. I've done lots of research in brothels.

There was a novel a few years ago, Brass, by Helen Walsh, in which the female protagonist tries to sleep with prostitutes, and virtually no one will see her. There's one who just doesn't care, but generally there are all these rules—I won't do that, I won't sleep with women.

When I went to brothels, as a woman, all the men would think I was a prostitute. I would get offers. The brothel owners would always tell me to come at six in the evening, before business started. The atmosphere was so nice. They were all completely naked and had high heels, and it was so warm, everybody was sweating. And just walking in the entrance area in the bar, it's just like paradise. People are naked and sexual and humid. And I thought, it's a big shame that we don't have that for women. There is such a nice range for men, they have so much opportunity—porn on the Internet, wanking booths. But women have nothing.

Helen is not a hippie, even though she celebrates her "naturalness." She's very modern. But do you think men who say they prefer their women totally shaved, with artificial breasts, is it because of a kind of familiarity with porn, or is it what they want?

Of course all the shaving stuff comes from porn, and I think that often men don't have enough self-confidence to admit that they would like a non-shaven woman. For example, women with pubic hair in porn would be the perverted corner, complete fetish, a niche like pregnant women or ninety-year-olds.

I hate shaving, but I shave because I want to be an attractive woman and I don't want people to throw stones at me in the street. But I think there would be a much wider range of possibilities if people talked to each other more. There are men who wouldn't give a fuck if their wife was shaven or not, so she wouldn't have to bother. Nearly all prostitutes are completely shaven, and men go there and think that this is the fashion, but maybe they don't all like it. A completely shaven pussy looks really weird. I just don't want all women to be the same. Why do we all have to shave the same way? Some women would look much nicer with a little bit of hair.

Ariel Levy has this idea of "raunch culture," where porn and the stripper image of women has come to be seen as the only image of womanhood worth aspiring to.

Heterosexual women and men are both equally bad. Men don't stand up for what they like, because there's a pressure on men that they have to like these fully shaven women. A man wouldn't dare to say in the pub, "Look, I really like women with big bushes." But women are so hard on themselves, like, "Oh no, I can't have sex, my tummy is too fat and my tits are too small." And it's not fun to have sex with women who are insecure about their bodies.

For me, it's the same. I keep thinking I have to stop eating this, and stop drinking beer. It's unhealthy thinking. If I'm being really honest, on the one hand I want women to be liberated, but on the other, I have terrible problems. I think I'm too fat, although I'm probably too thin. It's really difficult, for example, to live in a society like this with small tits. I don't even believe my husband when he says he likes the way I look. He has to tell me ten times a day and I still don't believe him. I think he wants to fuck a blonde, big-titted lady. You run around and you have complexes about everything. It's so difficult to keep it out of your head.

So how does Helen manage it?

That's why she exists! She's like my brave, freed alter ego. I can be like her sometimes, but only verbally.

I think some of the negative readings of your book argue that it can't be a feminist novel because Helen isn't totally strong, that she's not fully mentally sound.

The problem with political ideas like feminism is that you are not allowed sometimes to say the truth. In Germany we have lots of older, very famous feminists. And it is not allowed for me, as a young feminist, to say that women are masochistic. I am and all my female friends are. We stand in front of the mirror, we are naked, and we feel ugly as fuck. We see everything as wrong. We try and fight our body to become prettier and work on it. It's not at all free and self-confident. I don't want it to be like that, but I see that it is.

This interview first appeared in Salon and is reprinted here by permission of Nina Power, author of the book, One-Dimensional Woman.

About the Author:
Charlotte Roche was born in England in 1978 and raised in Germany, where she still resides with her husband and daughter. A longtime presenter on *Viva*, the German equivalent of MTV, she is a well-known and award-winning television personality. *Wetlands* is her first novel.

About the Translator:
Tim Mohr is a staff editor at *Playboy* magazine. His writing has also appeared in other publications, including *The New York Times*. Prior to joining *Playboy*, he spent six years as a club DJ in Berlin. His translation of *Guantanamo*, by Dorothea Dieckmann, won the Three Percent Prize for best translation of 2007.

The translator wishes to thank Andrej Huesener for his advice and his careful read of the draft manuscript.